THE SECRET TOWER

By the same author

Dark Flame
Stormy Heritage
Destiny's Daughter
Portrait of a Girl
Mistress of Blackstone
Merlake Towers
Tarnefell
Folly's End
Forest Heritage
Castle Carnack
Heronsmere
The Tregallis Inheritance
Trenhawk
Return to Carnecrane
Carnecrane

Ghost Stories:
Haunted Waters
The Haunted Garden
Chill Company
The Dark Land
The Dark God
Ghostly Carnival
The Haunted Valley
They Walk at Twilight
Unseen Footsteps
Where No Birds Sing
Where Phantoms Stir
Whisper in the Night

The Secret Tower

MARY WILLIAMS

WILLIAM KIMBER

First published in 1988

British Library Cataloguing in Publication data

Williams, Mary
The secret tower
I. Title
823′.914 [F]

ISBN 0-7183-0695-3

William Kimber & Co Ltd is part of the
Thorsons Publishing Group, Wellingborough,
Northamptonshire, NN8 2RQ, England.

Photoset in North Wales by
Derek Doyle & Associates Mold, Clwyd.
Printed in Great Britain by
Billing & Sons Limited, Worcester

1 3 5 7 9 10 8 6 4 2

For Amy with love

Introduction

Because of my deep love for Wales – especially the southern areas bordering England – I have written this novel of romantic and warring passions set against the mysterious Black Mountains, hoping to capture on paper a little of their magic which to me has always been unique and compelling.

Although factual details of history appear here and there, the story and characters are entirely fictional, as are Llangarrack itself and the mountain valley I have chosen to invent and depict. The period portrayed is the mid-nineteenth century, and I sincerely hope any true Welsh historian who chances to see it will not grudge the slight licence I have taken in juggling harmlessly at times geographically with real places, and those created in my own mind, for the sake of the plot.

For many years of my life I lived in Wales, and though Cornwall also is strongly in my blood and heart, there are times when I ache once more to be standing on a high ridge overlooking the humped peaks of Gwent and Breconshire, watching the morning mists slowly lift to reveal the magic splendour of that special stretch of Britain, or in the evening as the dying sun sends transient shadows streaking down the lonely slopes.

One day perhaps I will write a more serious and longer work dealing with the area. *The Secret Tower* is just a story which I hope nevertheless will be enjoyed by the uncritical, and by some who may feel as I do, possessing a mystical love of mountains which is either inborn in one or not.

Mary Williams

I

I was packed up and despatched like a parcel of goods, to be delivered to a strange address.

In just that way.

One moment I had been chatting with Polly the postmistress in her small shop where she sold everything from stamps, string, newspapers and sugar sweets from glass jars to boot polish and aniseed drops – oh, everything you could think of – and the next I noticed from the window a vehicle halt at the terraced house opposite where I lived with my foster-mother, who was a minister's widow, Mrs Price.

A man got out and rapped on the door. He was very large and tall, wearing a black cape and high stove hat. A second later Mrs Price's long, sad face appeared – I always called her Mrs Price, never 'mam', although I had lived with her since she'd had me from the foundling home when I was about five years old. There was a nodding and speech between the two – a pause while the stranger disappeared through the door, followed by the bustling figure of Mrs Price hurrying across the road to fetch me.

She looked anxious and a little strained, saying, in her usual autocratic dry voice, 'Are you tidy then? Is your apron clean? Come, girl. Tie your hair back. Important it is you should please the fine gentleman.'

I wanted to say, 'Why should I please that strutting large stranger? Haughty he looks, not my kind at all.'

But I held my tongue, as I'd been taught to do during my eleven years with the Widow Price. Oh, yes, during that time I'd learned good manners, and how to appear meek and good when I really wasn't, because after all I was only a foundling child from an orphanage with no known parents of my own; therefore, as the Widow Price had pointed out insistently, what I lacked in honourable birth and breeding must be minimised as much as possible through polite behaviour, virtuous thoughts, a modest exterior, and by remembering always how grateful I should be to the good Lord for giving me an early chance of developing to useful womanhood.

The 'chance', I realised, referred to her care of me, the 'useful womanhood' to obey some husband picked for me by my legal guardians. Who those guardians were I'd never known, but my foster mother had more than once informed me that by the time I'd passed my sixteenth birthday I must be prepared for married life. Until then, I would have a period of tuition at the Dame School, leaving at thirteen to spend my days supervised by herself, in that manner becoming educated for domestic duties which would include, of course, the arts of sewing sheets and embroidering samplers in designs of religious verses, flowers and birds. Cleaning and more menial tasks would also be my lot because, the Widow Price said, every woman worth her salt should know the right way to run a house, whether she had servants or not.

So it was that I became primed for wifehood ahead.

My foster-mother indeed was strict, but not unkind to me, although I had little contact out of school with young companions; most of the schoolchildren were those of mining families, one or two of the farming community. Of the first section, a number left when they were but nine years old to follow their brothers and fathers at the pit. Although the Widow Price prayed in their company at the Methodist Church twice every Sunday, I was made to feel from my earliest years at Nanty-Clyd, that I belonged subtly to a different sphere of society, was a little apart; not *above* – Mrs Price, being a good Christian, would sternly have denied such distinctions, for were we not 'all God's creatures and therefore of equal worth'?

Despite such a noble philosophy, however, her whole attitude where I was concerned was to keep me from 'mixing' in any familiar way. The fact that I had been taught to speak English as fluently as Welsh, helped her objective a good deal, the popular opinion in those parts being that the Welsh language came first always in Wales – English merely to be endured for educational and utilitarian purposes.

Only the Rhys-Evans children had been approved of by my foster-mother as suitable companions. Their home was a small farm some way up the mountain, and although the three elder sons, Evan, Daffyd and Idris, worked down the mine, their father, Thomas, was a mining engineer which gave him a status above ordinary workers; also his wife, Ann, was quite a scholar and had been a schoolteacher before her marriage. Her brother, Dai, looked after the few animals and grew the minimum of crops necessary, helped by Ann, who made butter which was much appreciated at the village shop. Oh, they were a contented household and I was permitted to visit there, becoming friendly with Bryn and Marged, the youngest of the family.

Especially Bryn.

He was a year older than myself, and Marged a year younger. Both had brown curly hair, creamy gold skins, and the dark eyes of the true Celt. But Marged's eyes were sparkling and open, brimming with mischief and the hint of laughter, whereas Bryn's were softer, filled with dreams. He could be merry too, though. No one could enjoy life more than Bryn, but it was the thoughts, a certain withheld quality behind the steady gaze, that entranced me. In a subtle way, I felt, he was different from the rest, which gave us much in common; and as we grew older I learned a good deal about that inner self which drew us closer still.

He would not go down the pit, he told me; knowledge was what he wanted – to know all about people, and books, and maybe, if he was lucky, he would somehow get a scholarship to college and teach as his mother, Ann, had done. Yes, maybe that was possible, or perhaps he'd choose to travel like the Englishman, George Borrow, and write his adventures down later. Not that he admired the English in every way. But they were clever enough to have taken Welsh territory in the past, and to have explored half the world. It would be fine to travel, he thought, so he could return to the old mountain with new passion and fire in his veins for what was surely the grandest place on earth.

How he loved the mountain.

So did I, especially to the east where winding tracks led upwards between heathered clumps and gorse, away from the smoke and minestacks of the valley to the high ridge overlooking the distant misty peaks of the Brecon Beacons. Sometimes Ann gave us a packet of sandwiches on special occasions, so we could climb to the top and eat there after our walk.

Sheep, the small sturdy kind, would dot the hillside, and tiny mountain pansies starred the short turf. The wind would be fresh and sweet on our faces, and happiness radiated everywhere, because I was alone with Bryn, and imagined a future when I could be his wife and with him always.

It seemed impossible then that I could really be sent away to some strange place where I'd be married to a man I didn't know. Whether Bryn had the same idea I wasn't sure. But his hand was warm on mine sometimes, and his eyes could be very serious, although he said nothing. In his way, I suppose, he was a bit of a poet, and therefore shy. But there was a rugged quality about him, too, a vitality and zest for knowledge concerned with studying and writing – but with a determination to live physically as well, with all the lusty life that was in him.

Those were good days, those days of innocence before the awakening. That is how I think of it – the 'Awakening'. And there was no particular reason I can think of now, why it should have come so suddenly just when it did, like the bursting of a radiant sun around us, except that we were alone, and free, and a small blue butterfly rested on my neck before Bryn kissed it.

Oh, how beautiful it was, our coming together, with our bodies close and warm and sweet, and all the scents and secret murmurings of nature around us.

Sundays afterwards I prayed silently in Chapel to the good Lord, not for forgiveness, for surely there was nothing to forgive, but that my foster-mother shouldn't find out. The weeks passed. So far no one guessed, not even Bryn, until I told him what I knew by then was true, and that I was with child. He was shocked, of course, then sorrowful and worried.

'Are you sure? Really *sure*?' he asked. 'Perhaps it's a mistake.'

'No,' I'd answered. 'I'm sure. And I don't mind. I'm glad, *glad* to have something of *yours*, Bryn – ours, together. Just think –' I broke off suddenly, arrested by the look on his face, bewilderment changing to a kind of fear, of non-acceptance that added years momentarily to his youth, making a man of him before his time; a man defeated by the bitterness of hard experience. So he might appear when he was forty.

A wave of doubt filled me. Gone was the wild hope and magic of the day. I'd forced myself to believe everything would be all right, choosing a moment to speak when the morning was glistening with first dew under the rising sun, and the young undergrowth thrusting pale green and gold through last years bracken. But now – 'Bryn,' I said, clutching both his shoulders hard and close, 'don't look like that. Aren't you, can't you be pleased? Just a little, Bryn. I know it's early, too soon perhaps, but – but – we could be married –'

Very firmly he removed my hands and stepped back facing me and shaking his head slowly. Gradually the hard lines of his mouth softened but his eyes remained narrowed, as though seeing me properly for the first time.

'You don't understand one bit, do you, Cariad?' he said, with wondering despair in his voice.

'Understand?' I echoed mechanically.

'What it would be like, bringing an unwanted child into the world? Being chained and frustrated even before we'd begun to live?'

He turned his head away defiantly, staring with chin out-thrust to the sky. '*No.* I'm sorry. Oh, hell, yes. I'm sorry, Olwen, it's not for me. Not yet.'

'You mean – you don't love me?'

'Love?' He gave a soft short laugh as though the word meant nothing. 'Yes. But there are other things a man has to have, one like me. And it doesn't last forever, what we have now, you and me. Time changes folk. Imagine it – me slaving myself to the bone in the valley on a mere pittance, just to see you becoming a drab, overworked and tired, and everyone knowing how Bryn Rhys-Evans had lain with Widow Price's Olwen and had to wed her because of it.'

'It wouldn't matter to me what folk said, and I was your wife –'

'I'm not wanting a wife. In ten years' time, maybe. I'm sorry, Cariad, but that's how it is.'

'I see.' Even in my own ears my voice sounded helpless, dreary.

'Look!' He turned round quickly and came back towards me, taking me by the arms and staring relentlessly into my eyes. They were still Bryn's eyes, I remember telling myself, but different. No longer fresh and glowing as mountain pools with the sun of them, but hard with the clarity of ice, and cold in fear. 'The way's clear for you, Olwen – for both of us. In a few weeks – didn't you say, it was weeks? – he comes for you, doesn't he? This man marked out for you? That's what you said. Well, then, you'll take him and make the best of it.'

'But how *can* I, like this? He'd notice. I –'

'The Widow hasn't, nor others. And when you're safely wed the child'd be his anyway. Premature –'

It was at that moment all the love I'd had for Bryn turned suddenly to such bitterness and contempt I could have struck him.

Instead, I just turned and walked away, with my head high, though I was trembling and my heart thudding sickeningly in my ears.

Down the mountain path I went, not looking back, out of his life forever.

And that's how I came to be leaving 'Polly the post's' shop that far away late spring afternoon to meet the forbidding-looking man chosen by my guardians, the 'authorities', to be my husband.

I did my best to appear outwardly calm and dignified, knowing that it would be to my advantage to do so. But inside resentment and fear tightened into a hard knot of tension.

He was standing with his back to the window when I entered Widow Price's sitting room, so I did not see his features clearly until he turned his head partially to greet me.

He was stern-looking, and dark – not ugly, or stout or very old, as he might have been – but hard, with a scar under one cheekbone resembling a cleft in a countenance carved of stone.

'So you're Olwen,' he said after a perceptible pause. His voice was emotionless, giving no hint of approval or criticism. Neither did he hold out a hand.

I was quite aware that my foster-mother expected me to bob or give a little curtsey. She had primed me many times on the matter. But now the moment had come I couldn't bring myself to do it. He was, after all, destined to be my husband unless I could somehow extricate myself from such a forbidding future, and whatever he thought of me, it was very important he should recognise I was not without pride. So I bowed my head briefly, and said, 'Yes, sir.'

'Well,' he resumed, 'there's no point on wasting words, since we shall have plenty of time ahead for any necessary discussion. I'm informed by your foster mother, Mrs Price here, that you have been well schooled in the practical duties of wifehood, and your status to be in my household.'

For a moment I couldn't bring myself to answer. If I'd spoken it would have been in a torrent of words crying, 'I know nothing, *nothing*. Only that I don't want to marry you. It's all been arranged – and if it wasn't for Bryn and what he's done to me, the baby, I'd run away now. Run away somewhere into the mountains where you couldn't find me. I don't like you. I don't like anything about you. The thought of lying with you like I did with Bryn is *hateful*.'

But my lips remained cold and tight, until I heard Mrs Price's harsh whisper in my ear saying, 'Answer the gentleman. Remember your manners.'

I swallowed hard and replied mechanically, 'I understand.'

'Sir.'

'*Sir*,' I repeated loudly and clearly, thinking how undignified having to show such formal obeisance to a man destined so shortly to be my husband.

'That's all right then,' he remarked with a trace of relief in his manner that relapsed from cold formality into casual indifference. He turned his gaze once more upon Mrs Price.

'I will leave you now,' he remarked, 'to pack any clothes and female accessories you've prepared, and in an hour's time –' he glanced at the heavy watch hanging from a gold fob strung across his waistcoat – 'I take it you'll need no longer.'

'Oh, no, Master Geraint, sir,' the Widow Price exclaimed with a hint of flurry in her voice. 'No, no! everything is ready. I can assure you –'

'Good!' he interrupted. 'We have some miles to travel before we reach Brecon where a simple ceremony will be performed. After that we shall go straight on to Llangarrack. I've no fancy for wasting time and money at any fancy hotel or bawdy inn. So I'll go now, I have a little business to attend to hereabouts and will return in that time.'

'Without refreshment or a sup of wine, sir?'

'I've no need of it,' he said curtly, and quite rudely, I thought, because I knew some best brandy had been kept ready for the occasion. I had learned also, from what I'd seen of the ordinary men and miners of our village that a taste of spirits could do much to mellow the temper on occasion, and I wished very much – oh, how I wished during those first moments of awesome, even frightening, contact, that I could be given a glimpse of friendliness, some sign that beneath the cold exterior was a spark of human warmth and feeling.

I could sense none, and could only retain an air of composure by closing my eyes briefly and clenching my cold fists against my sides. He obviously noticed.

'She looks tired,' I heard him say. 'Nothing wrong with her health, is there?'

While the Widow Price tried to reassure him I was remembering suddenly, with anguish, the gentle but firm strength of Bryn's arms round me, the sweet tangy scent of heather as he kissed me, and the wide expanse of open sky above the mountain, where the blue butterflies hovered, oblivious of the smoke and mine works of the valley far below.

Oh, Bryn, I thought, why have you left me to this terrible thing, to the mercies of a hard ruthless stranger who doesn't even like me? We could have managed, I know we could.

But Bryn wanted a world I didn't know and never would. He had always been a great one in his passion for Wales. But neither Wales nor I had been enough when it came to the test.

Adventure and gold. Oh, yes, I had to face the truth. Such was Bryn's hope. His love for me had merely been a passing thing. Perhaps if I could have offered him my dowry – but there would have been none if we'd married without the consent of my mysterious guardians.

How I resented them, and their ability to keep me a pawn in their own game without kith or kin of my own to turn to!

Who was I? Where had I been born? And what strange circumstances had driven me as a baby to the orphanage and later to the Widow Price's home where I was to grow up without a clue to my real identity or those of my parents?

It was so unfair. Anger stirred in me and brought me suddenly to a swift decision. Whatever happened, and however difficult my strange new life with Master Geraint proved to be, I would face it with pride. Yes. I would be proud. After all – my imagination leaped in that short interval to wild possibilities – I *could* be the daughter of a noble household, stolen perhaps as a baby by gypsies, and left later on the steps of some cottage or institute. Or – or – oh, there were so many exciting avenues leading to my present circumstances. The biggest puzzle of all, though, was why I should have guardians and a dowry at all.

My fancies were broken by Mrs Price's harsh voice saying, 'Wake up, girl. Master Geraint is leaving. This is no time for day-dreaming.'

I pulled myself together and the next moment the thin, strong hand of my future husband took my own for a second. It was pulsing with life, and a little shiver chilled my spine, with apprehension of the unknown.

A moment later Mrs Price was seeing him from the sitting room into the hall. A brief few words were passed, followed by the sharp slam of the front door. I glanced automatically towards the window, and saw his dark reflection pass to the waiting vehicle. Then the Widow Price returned, with a firm authoritative set to her chin.

'You were not very polite,' she said sharply. 'It's understandable, of course, you should be a little nervous. But you're a lucky girl, Olwen, to have such a fine Welsh gentleman willing to accept a foundling child for wife. Try and remember that my dear –' her voice had perceptibly softened, 'and you'll find it easier to adjust to your new circumstances.'

I suppose in her way she had become fond of me, and just for a moment I was tempted to put the forbidden query: 'Why am I being married off like this? Who were my parents?'

But as though sensing what was in my mind she continued briskly. 'Now, enough dilly-dallying. We've no time to waste, and that is so indeed. Come along then and we'll pack together. Two heads are better than one.'

There was very little actually to pack. The underwear, flannel petticoats and cotton skirts, were already laid in the one light trunk reserved for the purpose. The two day dresses I owned – simple but good, were pressed and flat in the wardrobe drawers waiting, and the gown specially made for me by the Widow's own hands for the special occasion ahead, bluish-grey embroidered with dark ribbon and demurely styled, was packed between tissue paper in a cardboard box of its own. It was waisted and high-necked, boned and not really comfortable, keeping my chin high for dignity's sake, allowing only a slight inclination of the head to indicate submission to my future husband's wishes.

I was laced into tightly fitting corsets which gave no indication of my already slightly swelling breasts. In the gown I felt stifled and repressed. My hair was drawn severely from my face and coiled in plaits high at the back of my head. The underskirts of my bridal outfit were so heavy that after the first quarter of an hour my body ached.

Seeing my solemn set expression, the Widow Price said, '*Do* be a little more cheerful, girl. Just look at your face. You might be contemplating a funeral instead of a wedding.'

I felt like it. And when I saw my expression through the mirror I realised she was quite right. Sullen full mouth, grey eyes staring cold and unblinkingly, under thick black lashes and rather heavy brows. I managed a faint smile, at the same time forcing the frown away. I looked different, almost plain – not at all the same girl who'd lain with Bryn in the wild thyme and heather, hair tangled in dew, my heart and whole being brimful with love and sunshine and all the promise of a lifetime together.

'That's better,' my foster mother said unconvincingly. 'You don't want Master Geraint to change his mind at the last moment and decide he doesn't want you, do you? Men don't like sullen women.'

Then perhaps he won't like *me*, I told myself hopefully. If he didn't, what would happen? Should I be sent back ignominiously to the Widow Price? Or could I be foisted off on to some other unknown man wanting my dowry, one even more unpleasant than Master Geraint?

The very idea was sufficient to keep me quiet and apparently acquiescent. It was quite true, I thought

desperately, important that the grim Master of Llangarrack should find my looks agreeable, especially considering the inevitable shock awaiting when he discovered
my condition.

I suddenly felt faintly sick and shivered.

'Whatever's the matter with you, girl?' Mrs Price
demanded, noticing the colour draining from my face. 'Is
it unwell you are? You've not taken a chill, have you?
There's been far too much wandering about the mountain
recently insufficiently clad. Spring days can be treacherous. It would be unpleasant indeed if you greeted your
fine new husband with a snuffle and snivel. Come now. I'll
get you a draught –'

'No, thank you,' I interrupted, recovering. 'It's nothing.
And I don't want a draught.'

'Oh! Very well.' She sounded annoyed. 'Here's your
cloak then. Put it round you. Master Geraint will expect
everything to be punctual. And see your hair's well tucked
beneath the bonnet. That froth of veiling alone is frivolous
enough to satisfy a man of taste.'

I sighed, and did as I was bid.

Presently, when the last few knick-knacks were packed
into my trunk, and my reticule equipped with the small
etceteras considered necessary for a young woman bound
for an important journey, the cab arrived at the door of
the only real home I had ever known, and I was being
ushered through the narrow hall while the driver came to
collect my luggage.

The Widow gave me a quick embarrassed peck of a kiss
on one cheek – she had never been one for showing her
feelings – and a minute later I found myself in the landau
seated beside the upright stove-hatted figure of Master
Owain Geraint – someone I already disliked, but whose
attentions I was steeled to endure for the sake of security
and the unborn child I was carrying.

In spite of my unnatural rather loveless childhood and

disillusionment over Bryn, a wave of sadness flooded me as the vehicle clattered down the familiar cobbled street of Nanty-Clyd, past grey rows of houses, identical except for curtained windows and the grim-looking Methodist Chapel facing the public house opposite. The threat of tears had almost choked me as Polly the Post's sturdy figure waved from the step of her shop.

The small town held no beauty except that of familiarity and the kindness of its inhabitants. Yet that kindness had somehow penetrated the greyness and grim reality of hard-earned livelihood down the pits, giving a sad dignity that I would remember always; I knew that – a dignity creating longing and fulfilment in song. Oh, yes. However strange my new life as the wife of Master Geraint might be, I would never forget the sounds of singing from 'The Dragon Inn' on a Saturday night, or the full-throated choirs swelling the air from Church or Chapel on Sundays.

Whether the hard-faced man seated next to me sensed any of my sad emotions I don't know. He showed nothing and said little during the lonely drive towards Brecon except stilted remarks such as 'everything will be very different for you at Llangarrack, but I hope your admirable foster mother was right when she assured me you were of an adaptable nature.'

'I shall do my best,' I answered.

'Hm!'

After that there was a long pause, a silence unbroken except for the clip-clop of horses' hooves and the rattle of wheels. Nanty-Clyd was soon left behind and the familiar fading silhouette of the mountain at the back of us. No longer were the dark shapes of the smoky mine-works visible looming over the valley streets; instead, the countryside at times appeared completely deserted, except for a shepherd's hut or farmstead appearing round a corner of a lane. The constant jogging up and down hills released some of my tension, giving place to sleepiness and a sense of unreality like that of slumbering in some fantastic dream. A faint spring mist distorted hedges, wreathing the occasional hamlets of our route into sombre grey. Everything about me felt grey – myself, my future, and the stern upright silhouette of the stranger at my side. He hardly moved or glanced at me; it was as though my presence was already distasteful to him. Once, when the landau jerked unpleasantly over some obstruction, a piece of rock or large stone, he muttered under his breath angrily, alerting me to sudden full consciousness.

I turned sharply to look at him. His profile jutted aggressively, jaws tight, underlip set. A bold, overbearing, quite handsome-looking man in a rugged way, I thought, though at that moment forbidding and frightening.

Perhaps I shivered, I don't know. He looked at me and asked, 'Are you cold? Take this rug if you are.' He removed it from his knees and pressed it against my shoulder.

'Thank you,' I said, 'but I don't need it.'

'Then don't act as if you did,' he said shortly. 'I can assure you your life will hold many a harder bump than a mere jolt from a horse's stumble.' When I didn't reply he added as an afterthought, 'I presume you like horses?'

'I've had nothing to do with them,' I told him bluntly.

'Do you mean you don't *ride*?' I sensed scorn and irritation in the query.

'The Widow Price had no horses,' I answered. 'I'd no chance to learn.'

'Then you'll soon have to,' he commented. 'Existence at Llangarrack is isolated, and you'll be expected to help in many ways.'

'I understand,' I answered, which was not true; I understood nothing nor could I visualise anything clearly about my existence ahead of the remote wild place I was headed for. My only consolation was that there would be mountains. Not like the familiar high ridge overlooking

Nanty-Clyd, of course; and there would be no mines working below probably – no Polly the Post, or choirs to stir the air. And no Bryn. Master Owen Geraint, as the Widow Price had clearly indicated, was a 'gentleman', a Welsh gentleman, with a large estate and country house, in which I was to be mistress. Contemplating my position, fear once again tautened in me. I already sensed he was a proud man, with a temper – a man who could be violent if driven to it, perhaps even kill. And when he found out about me, about the trick played on him – for he'd surely consider it so – 'Oh, God,' I thought, 'let something happen to stop this terrible marriage, and dear Lord, please help me not to have such awful thoughts.'

But maybe God and the Good Lord weren't listening: because it happened.

When we reached Brecon in the late afternoon, Master Geraint and I were married at a tiny Methodist Chapel by a fierce-looking minister dressed all in black, who conducted the short service in Welsh. I was trembling as my new husband, whom I already intensely disliked, placed the ring upon my finger. He didn't appear to notice, but after an indifferent glance at my hand, looked away again, inclined his head slightly towards the sombre cleric, who produced the register for us to sign.

It was strange writing 'Olwen March' for the last time – 'March' because it had been the month those sixteen years ago when I'd been taken to the orphanage, and given that surname. Later, of course, when I'd joined Mrs Price I'd generally been referred to by the natives as 'the Widow Price's girl', which I'd very soon got used to.

Now, again, I was someone quite different – Olwen Geraint, wife of Owain Geraint, landowner of Llangarrack.

I could hardly believe it; I felt in a dream – an unreal world, from which I presently must wake as the vehicle, following the short ceremony, took the numerous turns in the direction of the distant humped rim of high lands rising against the fading sky. A thin mist enhanced the illusion, giving ethereal beauty to the lonely Welsh border country which merged eventually on one side to the flatter landscape of Herefordshire and forests of Gloucestershire.

'Gradually land has been taken from us which should be Welsh,' Master Geraint said once. 'And you must never forget your own nationality. The English are covetous; therefore, we have no liking for them except when it is to our advantage to appear so. Still, you are not likely to contact any except when I see fit. Visitors to Llangarrack are rare.'

'I understand.'

He glanced at me briefly.

'You seem to accept everything I say,' he remarked irritably. 'Have you no mind of your own?'

'Ys,' I retorted rashly. 'But until I know you better I think it's wise to agree with you. Mrs Price taught me to hold my tongue until I knew what was expected of me.'

Just at that opportune moment the landau gave a jolt that bumped us briefly against each other. My bonnet caught his shoulder. As I tried to adjust it, he said, 'Ah, let the silly thing be. We're not bound for a reception.'

After that little more was said until we reached the house Llangarrack, my future home.

*

In the early evening light my first impression was of a square, gaunt building hewn out of a rising rocky slab of mountain. We had left a hamlet crouched in woodland half a mile back, and taken a lane cutting upwards between humped brooding hills that grew taller and more forbidding under caps of mist as the valley narrowed. Across the pale thread of roadway squat humped trees flung distorted shadows, and occasionally branches tapped the carriage windows giving the eerie impression of covetous, clawing fingers.

The drive to the house took a sharp turn to the left, continuing for a short way up a steep incline. It was no more than a rough track marked by a few windblown sycamores, and the face of Llangarrack showed a single lighted window staring like a square watchful eye from the stone walls. The land behind appeared inhospitable and barren.

For the first time I actually shuddered, not from cold but acute tension and dread. So this was the the country mansion of the 'fine Welsh gentleman' I had married, I thought. And all around me were the massed hills, the Black Mountains that were reputed to be so beautiful.

I could, in those first few moments, sense no beauty, or hope for the future. I was no more than a prisoner brought to an alien region that already resented me, encroaching on every side by sentinels, immense elemental forces shaped from primeval times to guard their own territory.

Whether Owain Geraint was aware of my mood I couldn't tell. But just for a moment or two his voice had a tinge of kindness in it, as he said gruffly, 'I expect you're tired. Cheer up. When you've eaten and had a good night's rest you'll feel better.'

The landau drew to a halt at the porch of the building. The light from the window vanished, and the front door opened, revealing the squat form of a woman holding a lamp. Owain stepped down, and offered me a hand. I took it, and managed not to cringe at its strength.

'I've a fire going in the parlour, master,' the woman said as I followed my husband into a dark shadowed hall. 'And a meal with broth to warm your bones. Chilly it is these early spring nights, and you and the young lady tired as you must be after the long drive from Nanty-Clyd.'

'We're later than I'd meant,' Owain replied shortly, 'and

I'm sure my – my wife will appreciate a meal. This –'
introducing us, '– is Mrs Maddox, my housekeeper. Mrs
Maddox –' turning to the short sturdy figure who was
revealed in the flicker of lamplight as quite elderly, even old
' – meet your new mistress. She'll be of help to you from
now on in getting through all the work that's to be done. I've
already explained to her that no one is idle here.'

'Thank you, master.'

She made no bob or gesture of welcome, just a brief bow
of her head in acknowledgement. A feeling of isolation, of
being unwanted, swept over me. I was cold. It was as though
all feeling in me had been stilled. The air of the house was
chill; a brooding atmosphere of neglect and things long past
seemed to hug every alcove and doorway, intensifying the
archaic solemnity of ancestral portraits hanging in heavy
frames on yellowed walls. A wide staircase curved upwards
in the shape of an 'S' to shadowed landings above. Through
a tall stained glass window the last glow of quickly fading
twilight filtered its eerie stream over the worn, once-
luxurious carpeting and tapestries, giving ghostly greenish
life to the ancient legends depicted there.

'Come along,' I heard Owain saying impatiently. 'Dream-
ing you can be presently, when you've washed and eaten
and ridden yourself of that ridiculous outfit. Mrs Maddox
has the bedroom ready with a hot brick for your feet maybe.
You'll be sleeping alone tonight.'

'Oh! I –'

He gave a short laugh. 'So forget any fears you have for
nuptial celebrations. I've much to do, and no fancy at the
moment for wooing a frightened virgin.'

I could feel the colour rise quickly to my face. 'Sir – I –'

'Dammit, Olwen. I have a name, then use it, and don't
argue. Stir yourself. Mrs Maddox here must be longing for
her nightcap after the extra work she's had getting everything shipshape and ready.'

I pulled myself together abruptly. 'Of course. Thank you

for all you've done, Mrs Maddox.' I had no idea what it was – even the 'hot brick' was mere conjecture on Owain's part. But the woman's small tight mouth softened slightly into mollified lines. She was stolidly waiting a few yards' away, lamp held up in a plump hand. As we moved towards her she turned and mounted the first few stairs laboriously, pausing at a short curve beneath the window. She stopped briefly to get her breath then went on again, leading the little procession of my husband and myself with the man and boy heaving up the luggage behind.

When the door of the bedroom was opened I had a surprise. It was more pleasant than I'd anticipated though the furniture was of heavy mahogany, and the walls panelled in oak. A lamp was already lighted on the dressing table, and a fire burning in the grate under a marble surround. Heavy velvet curtains in a pleasant dark crimson shade had been drawn across the windows, and the carpet, though faded, was patterned with roses. From other small details discovered next morning, I realised that attempts had been made to brighten and enliven the interior. Or maybe this certain room had previously been kept just for occasional guests visiting Llangarrack. Whatever the answer, I was grateful for the comparative comfort, and the knowledge that for this first night, anyway, I would be on my own.

I was too tired to worry about the future any more. Perhaps, after all it would be bearable and I would be able to put the memory of Bryn out of mind. As for the baby! – but that was a problem I'd have to settle later.

I slept soundly that night.

And in the morning when I drew the curtains I had my first real glimpse of the Black Mountains.

II

When I faced the view from the bedroom window in the morning light I was seized by excitement and a kind of wonder. Above the thread of winding road the line of rising hills was tipped with gold from the early sun. Mountains, yes. But without the stark mine works or smoke darkening the valleys below those of Nanty-Clyd. These rose from clustered trees brightly splashed with spring green, where a curling stream intertwined the undergrowth. Dark blue and purple shadows filled bowled recesses of ancient rock. A narrow, exciting, mysterious valley. For those first few moments fear and apprehension in me died. Oh, surely life could be good in this lovely place!

A new beginning; with high summer ahead.

And then I remembered.

Remembered Owain, and the plight I was in – the daunting news I had to confess when evening came, and we faced each other, man and wife.

I turned and went back to the washstand reluctantly, where a basin and ewer stood ready for me with a towel and water to wash from. The water was cold. I'd thought, perhaps, a can of hot might be brought up to me by the housekeeper or some servant if any more were employed there. Such a vain thought, which I realised a moment later. Mr Geraint, my husband, had emphasised during the short conversations we'd had that everyone at Llangarrack was expected to work and had made it obviously clear that there would be no exceptions in my case.

In spite of my dowry, I thought bitterly – whatever it was. My own ignorance of its worth and source stirred new rebellion in me. I would do what was necessary in the house, and as much as possible that could be expected of me in the role of Owain's wife. But servant I would *not* be. A bargain had been concocted which was none of my making. I'd been but a pawn in a calculating game. Ironically it occurred to me that so had he, ignorant as he was of my condition.

Like a dark shadow the knowledge of what lay ahead shattered my temporary flare of confidence. He would have to know the truth. Almost three months had passed since that fatal day of my 'awakening' when I'd laid with Bryn in the heather above Nanty-Clyd. Even if I wished to I would not possible be able to delude Master Geraint – he was still 'master' to me – that the coming child could possibly be his.

I shivered.

I was frightened again.

How would he react when he discovered the truth? Beat me, perhaps, or worse? Perhaps cast me out as a criminal minus a penny of my own to make my own way back to the Widow Price in disgrace.

Or kill me?

Men had been known to do great violence when betrayed by a woman. Was he such a man? No, I did not really think so, although I could imagine a whip about my back. That cold relentless face and dark narrowed eyes suggested a ruthless personality unlikely to show mercy or understanding in such a sorry situation. At the best, he would be affronted and furiously angry.

I had an impulse somehow to speak to him tentatively during the day about the matter, and so soften the blow.

But the hours were too filled by being told what was

what, of introductions to farm workers, and domestic staff, which, apart from the old housekeeper, consisted only of a girl and a boy – of being taken round the rambling house, dairy and kitchens – where I was told meals were taken these days to save expense of heating and time – for any intimate conversation.

As time passed dreariness encompassed me, tinged with despair. The atmosphere was chill and joyless, overhung by an air of thrift and dedication to work that excluded any sense of comfort or possible joy.

Outside was so different; all green and gold over the hills and stone-walled fields. Birds sang, I supposed, from the hedges and wooded valleys beneath the mountains; but I did not hear them. In a miserable daze I heard Owen saying, 'You will see to it that the house is clean from now on, and assist Mrs Maddox in the dairy. I shall expect you to be comely and polite when anyone comes to dine – which is very rare these days. We eat in the dining room then; on such occasions you'll be responsible for an acceptable, well-cooked meal, as economically put on as possible. At times, your assistance may be required on the land. There are many jobs a healthy woman can do if she has a will for it. And I was assured by the Widow Price that you were never sick. She was speaking the truth, I hope?'

'Oh, yes,' I answered mechanically. 'I'm strong.'

'Good. There's no room for extravagance here.'

'So I've already been told,' I answered, a little pertly perhaps.

'Hm!'

After that there was silence between us for a time as we made our way down a rather damp and muddy track to the paddock and stables. We'd already inspected the kitchens and dairy, where I'd been informed the ageing Mrs Maddox would instruct me in the art of making butter and sterilising cream. The drive, which skirted a cobbled yard and cow-sheds, was damp and muddy also. It had rained in the night, and I had to lift my skirts with one hand in case they became dirtied at the hem. I was wearing my ordinary day dress under my cloak, which the Widow Price had considered suitable for morning use and light housework.

Owain glanced down at me critically. 'Those silly female things are ridiculous for seeing round a farm,' he said brusquely. 'You should be wearing stout sturdy boots.'

'I wasn't told I was coming to a farm,' I said, 'and I *am* wearing boots.'

'Those narrow pointed contraptions?' He laughed, but without humour. 'I can see you've a lot to learn. More than I guessed.'

'That's not my fault,' I told him hotly. 'I was told nothing about Llangarrack except that it was a country mansion with an estate. Mrs Price said –'

'Have done, girl. I'm not blaming you. Nor the Widow. And she was right about the house. A family home, the home of the Geraints it's been for centuries, with rich and profitable lands to sustain it. Many border battles were waged here. But –' he paused before adding, ' – bad times came. Political tricks and traitorous folk took much of our power and lands. So now it's my business to regain lost rights. And there's only one way to do it.' He was staring straight ahead. '*Work.* That's why every inch of ground must be utilised to the full. And mountain land isn't easy. Sheep? Yes – mountain sheep bring in a certain income. But besides sheep there should be cattle, a first rate herd. The best pastureland is there –' he pointed to a distant ridge – 'over the mountain. Once hundreds of acres of it belonged to the Geraints. Then it was taken.'

'Taken? How?'

'You're too quick with your questions,' he answered irritably. 'One day maybe you'll have knowledge of such things. You should know, though, that in spite of its great name, Llangarrack needs its farming for survival. And any man or woman who bides here has to work for his keep.'

I did not attempt at that point to question him further. He seemed determined to put me in my place, and once again apprehension – no, more than that – fear – chilled me when I thought of the night ahead.

All morning and throughout the afternoon until four o'clock, I was taken either tramping fields or being versed in my future duties which might well include, I'm told, having to take on the milking, should the need arise in a busy season. Only two men and one boy were employed for outside work and the girl, Dilly, was inclined to be clumsy.

'So as well as learning to ride a horse you'd better see to it that you get used to cows,' my husband said, with a quick sideways glance at me. 'And don't look so scared. Heaven help me – *and* you – if I've married a nit-wit.'

'I like animals,' I told him with as much enthusiasm as I could force into my voice. 'Only –'

'Yes?' The curt word made me reckless.

'If I'm to be milkmaid, cook, dairy girl, farm worker, housemaid and – and wife, as well as being at Mrs Maddox's beck and call, I can hardly be expected, can I, to act as hostess to any visitors you may have?'

My cheeks burned with rising indignation. I faced him very directly, and fancied I saw a quirk of amusement twitch his lips. Little fiery sparks of gold seemed to lighten his dark eyes. Then he shrugged, looked away, and said flatly, 'I don't see why not. Other women have done it in remote places like this. And I was informed you were a quick learner.'

I completely forgot caution and continued breathlessly, '*Other* women, *other* women. Oh, yes – in the days of slavery. But I'm not just 'other women', as you should understand, sir. I'm –'

'You're my *wife*.' From his tone and the hot colour in his face I knew he was finding it difficult to curb his quick temper, 'In case you had forgotten. However –' he paused before adding, 'that is a matter soon remedied. Tonight I shall have to see that you are fully aware of your true status.'

I bit my lip thinking, 'tonight will be awful. Tonight he has to know the truth. I should have been honest earlier and told Mrs Price. Oh, how I wish I'd done that. I'd have been sent away, of course – to the poorhouse perhaps – or I could have run off and tramped the roads. Anything – *anything* would have been better than to be at the mercy of this cruel man. Yes, he was cruel – I could sense it – as cruel as the hard rock of the mountains and the keen winds which in winter would sweep down the narrow valley. I could imagine the scene then, when summer was over, the greyness and frosted summits taken into icy mists. There would be snow there too, where sheep and lambs could be lost in the loneliness.

But it was wrong, surely, to have such fancies on a day when blossom still foamed, and the stream trickled merrily down the slopes. Almost like laughter it sounded, that rippling murmur of nature. Under different circumstances I could have laughed at myself, and lifted my arms happily to the clear sky, danced in the young feathery bracken as I'd danced for Bryn on the mountain above Nanty-Clyd. That had been before 'the awakening' of course, when I was innocent of life's fulfilment and what terrible joy and sadness it could hold. Looking ahead, I could see only misery with this harsh stranger who appeared to have no tenderness or consideration of my feelings.

So my mind went, this way and that, all through that tiring, seemingly endless first day.

Apprehension so gnawed me that I could hardly bring myself to eat, though the food, if simple, was good. During those sparse intervals I longed to rush from the kitchen to the bedroom and lock the door so for a few precious moments I could be alone. But the small shrewd eyes of Mrs Maddox were upon me, not unkindly perhaps, but ever watchful as though anxious to plumb my inmost thoughts. Owain gave me minimum attention at such times except to see no doubt that I left nothing on my plate. Yes, he would be like that, I told myself – mean, not condoning that a crumb at his table should be wasted, even though my stomach rebelled at the mutton stew and heavy greasy dumplings.

At supper, which was taken early by six-thirty – I had to excuse myself and rush upstairs to the washroom, overcome by a fit of nausea. Although the thought of returning to the meal was obnoxious, I did so as soon as I was capable, knowing that Owain would resent my absence.

He eyed me curiously when I entered the kitchen; as an excuse I'd placed my one shawl round my shoulders in case he asked the reason for my unexpected behaviour. But all he said was, 'Surely you weren't cold? See you're clad properly in future. The Widow Price should have made sure to it that you were properly equipped with the right kind of clothes for a working wife. We'll have to attend to that on the morrow. Maybe I'll ride over to Abergavenny. It's Market Day and possibly a roll of stout cloth or thick wool will be going at a reasonable price. Mrs Maddox is handy with the needle. She'll soon fit you up.'

I might by then have expected that kind of remark from him, but his obtuse callous way of talking and manner of discarding contemptuously the clothes Mrs Price had worked on with such care roused a streak of fury in me I'd not known I possessed.

How dared he? – how *dared* he?

I jumped up, and with flaming cheeks, cried, 'The clothes I have are quite warm and thick enough. All day I've done nothing but listen to orders, accept your criticisms and trudge through muddy fields and hear about duties and obligations, what I must do and wear, and I'm tired of it. *Tired*. Oh, leave me alone. *Leave* me.'

But it was I who left.

After sweeping the unwanted plate of food from the table, I rushed out with the sound and clatter of falling crockery and pottery in my ears, and returned to the bedroom once more where I lay, one hand on my stomach, breathing heavily, wondering wildly what would happen next.

After a time there was the sound of heavy footsteps on the stairs, and Owain came in. I'd forgotten to lock the door.

He stood by the bed looking down on me, and the gold sparks in his dark eyes were bright gleaming dots of flame. His mouth was hard.

'Don't you *ever* behave like that again,' he said, 'or you'll rue it. I warn you.'

When I said nothing he resumed:

'You'd better keep to your bed till I come to it. And when I do, let your manners be those of a dutiful wife and not of a wilful arrogant child.'

I remained silent. He turned on his heel then, striding to the door, left, and locked it behind him.

So I was prisoner.

My whole body trembled.

But there was nothing I could do. No way of escape. The window was high and narrow, and tightly shut, and the drop to the rocky ground below considerable.

All I could do was wait.

*

I was still lying on the bed when Mrs Maddox entered after a light knock. How long I'd been there I didn't know. Time had ceased to have meaning, swallowed up by the miasma of dread that encompassed me. Although I hadn't been aware of it, I must have been crying. My eyelids

smarted and felt swollen. She was carrying a cup of
something hot and said, not unkindly:

'Here, take this, and no arguing. It's overtired you are.
A drop of broth'll work wonders.'

I shook my head. 'Thank you. But I don't want it.'

Her mouth became pursed before she remarked
sharply, 'Stuff and nonsense. Now do as you're told. And
listen to me, young lady. The master may sound harsh, but
he's no use for tantrums and megrims in the house. Try
and behave as a grown-up woman should who knows her
place, and he'll make a fine husband. But if you act wild
and stubborn, he'll have his own way of taming you, and I
wouldn't envy you that. A lot on his mind he has, things
we'll not be talking about. So remember what I've said –
hold your tongue when he's edgy, and maybe this
marriage'll work out for you both. The master wants a son.
If you're clever you'll see he gets one. That's my advice.'

'Work out,' I thought when she'd gone. What a way to
talk, when her words only confirmed the bitter truth I'd
been wed to an overbearing autocrat with no use for a
woman but as a slave to his whims and to swell his purse.
Well, he'd had my dowry, whatever it had been. But
myself – my body? No. Bought I might have been; but he
was in for a shock. And I'd see he realised it the moment
he made an intimate move towards me. He'd soon know;
oh, yes, he'd soon know, I'd see to that.

A son! 'You shall have a son,' I said to myself, in no
doubt at all during those outraged moments of hardening
resolve that the unborn child I carried would be a boy.
'But he won't be yours, he'll be *mine*.'

The knowledge gave fire to my spirits until reaction set
in rousing dull fear.

It was later than I'd expected when he came, and I was
lying on the bed with my black hair loose, my already
swelling body clad only in a nightshift under the quilt. An
oil lamp cast a mellow glow round the dark walls and

heavy furniture. I closed my eyes against his approach. He moved close and touched one cheek with a finger. I flung him a brief glance and he laughed shortly. 'Still tired? I should have thought you'd had rest enough by now.'

I said nothing, but turned my face away. He walked to the mirror and stood staring a minute at my reflection shadowed through the glass, then gave a jerk to his neck-scarf and jacket, removing them before taking off boots and breeches.

I tried to still the wild thudding of my heart, saying to myself, 'It will soon be over now. In a few minutes I shall either be revenged or dead. And when he tries to ravish me –'

But my wild imaginings got no further, because he was there by the bedside, a magnificent specimen of manhood, quite naked, with a hot brilliant look in his eyes that I'd not seen before. And he didn't try to ravish me. He just laid one hand on my shoulder and said, 'There's nothing to be frightened of, Olwen. We're wed, remember? Come now, cariad, is it a brute you think me? I'll be gentle enough, if you give me the chance.'

He pulled down the quilt, and in a frenzy of bewilderment I swung myself over the other side of the bed and stood facing him, shivering not with chill or fear, but with emotions all mixed up that I couldn't understand at all.

He frowned. What softness there'd been in his expression turned slowly to stern scrutiny and a narrowing of eyes. I backed to a corner near the window. In four strides he was by me and had pulled the white shift from my shoulders, letting it fall to the floor. Just for a few moments nothing happened. The pause between was terrifying – more terrifying than any action could have been. Instinctively my right had travelled to the betraying curve of my stomach which must have been obvious in my starkness. I tried to look away, anywhere from the cold condemning stare fixed on me so ruthlessly.

But I could not.

It was as though hatred hypnotised and rooted me to the spot. Then I heard him say through clenched jaws and teeth in harsh undertones: 'So! it's no virgin I've married, no innocent young creature needing protection and gentle words. I'm surprised. I really *am*! Tell me, if you please, for you must have been aware of the trick you were playing, who first deflowered you? Who made mock of Owain Geraint to land him with a ripe young whore carrying a bastard child?' He came a foot closer and struck me sharply across the cheek. I flinched but gave no answer.

'Well?' he continued. 'Tell me. Or by God I'll *make* you. It's what you deserve – to be begging at my feet for mercy.'

'Very well, very *well*,' I cried heedlessly. 'But I'm no whore. I *loved* someone, yes. I know. I *know*. It was wrong of me perhaps. But you were nothing to me, *nothing*. Just a name given by the Widow Price occasionally. I didn't *want* to wed you, I never really thought it would happen. But then Bryn –'

'Ah. So his name is Bryn. What else?'

I shut my lips firmly before replying. 'Does it matter? He's no more to me now. He's – dead.'

Although in one sense the word was a lie, in a way it wasn't, for me he no longer existed except as a dream from the past without any tangible existence or bearing on my life.

'Hm!'

Owain turned on his heel, went to a chair, and sat on it with his head in his hands. I reached for my shift. He looked up quickly, picked it up and threw it at me.

His expression was bitterly set. There was the suggestion of a sneer about his mouth.

'Put it on. Cover yourself. The sight of you revolts me. And don't let me see you ever again displaying your wanton charms indecently clad or you'll smart for it. In the meantime you'll stay here, work for your keep, though I could throw you out here and now. After the brat's born –' he paused ' – we shall have to see, shan't we?' He gave a grim smile. 'Do you understand?'

I shook my head.

'Then you'd better start trying. Oh, don't worry. I've no fancy for secondhand goods at the moment. There's just one point I will make clear at the start of this extremely surprising and repugnant contract. When your byblow is born it can remain for two months – no more – under my roof. By that time a new home for it will have been found, and I shall make sure you never set eyes on it again.'

'But –'

'No "buts", and no conditions from you. I've been fooled, and that's the price of my own folly. Get you to bed now, and in the morning see you're modestly attired and ready for any tasks before you. I can assure you there'll be plenty.'

The next moment he was gone.

III

The next day it rained. So my time was spent mostly in the servants' quarters or being tutored by Mrs Maddox in household routine. Owain had left early for Abergavenny on some business project concerning agriculture, which was a relief to me since I was spared the embarrassment of having to face his hard, hostile stare. In the grey light the interior of Llangarrack appeared more unwelcoming and depressing even than I'd feared. Except for the large bedroom where I'd slept alone and the steamy kitchens and scullery the air was chill, the atmosphere gloomy and filled with dust. The wide main hall, staircase and vast reception rooms could once have been magnificent in years of prosperity, but meanness and struggle for survival had worn the carpets thin, and festooned certain locked premises of the house with a flim of cobwebs.

'Too much to do there is, just for that girl, Dilly, and an old body like me,' Mrs Maddox said, turning the key of the drawing room which had a musty smell of ancient velvet upholstery and curtains. 'When anyone important calls of course – which is a rare thing indeed these days – we have a real clear-up. But mostly this is shut *and* the large parlour.'

'Oh. I see.'

She flung me a dry glance.

'You don't, you know. You've no idea at all, *at all*, of what needs to be done at Llangarrack. Nor of the master either. But you'll learn, you'll learn. And if you're wise, girl –'

'I'm Mrs Geraint,' I reminded her pointedly, but with a faint smile. 'I realise it will be difficult for you, but perhaps it would be best to – to call me that – in front of Dilly, anyway. Oh, please don't think it conceited of me. It isn't that I want to air myself as mistress, and I'm grateful for your help and advice, and I hope we'll become good friends.' I paused before adding, 'It isn't easy for me. I didn't exactly *want* to come here.'

She shook her head and sighed, with the sigh very old people can have for the ignorance of the young. Then she said, with a tap on my shoulder, 'Maybe you didn't then. And you need have no fears I'll be dictatorial or wanting to rule the roost. There's only one ruler here and that's the master. I don't envy you, and that's a fact. It's glad I am to be giving up the domestic reins and I know full well how this marriage came about – arranged, as so many marriages are. So you needn't fret if anything bothers you. Just come to me and I'll give as comforting an ear as I can.'

I thanked her, and was truly grateful she bore me no ill will. I realised as the hours wore on that there was much more she could have told me of the circumstances concerning Owain's life, his past, and what he would expect of me.

'As I've already told you,' she remarked on that first dreary evening before Owain returned, 'you won't have much entertaining to do. Just the Triptons on occasion.'

Her voice had sunk to a low murmur that I fancied held a note of resentment. We were seated on a bench by a smouldering kitchen fire, drinking hot tea during a brief respite from the wearisome business of household inspections and chores. The rain had thickened, and was beating against the window in a constant tattoo of sound interspersed by the crackle of windblown twigs from an alder. Outside the mountains had receded into gloomy twilight. A small oil lamp cast a pale glow across the table throwing flickering shadows round shelves and walls.

'Triptons?' I queried.

She jerked a thumb to the window. 'Over the mountains – there. English. She? Well, a beauty in her way, I s'pose. But not my type. There was a time –' she broke off reminiscently with a shake of her head then relapsed into silence.

'Yes?' I enquired. 'What? You were saying –'

'Oh, nothing, *nothing*. Not *your* concern, or mine. But for the master's sake I very often think it would be better for him, far, if they were as many miles as could be away. Him, the husband, is very rich you see. Built a fine mansion over the ridge. Breeds horses and cattle, with thousands of acres of good pasture land that by rights should be Geraints'.'

'How? Why?' I enquired.

'Oh! something to do with an enclosure act which is too puzzling for me – and mixed up with a debt made by the master's elder brother before he was killed in the Crimea. He's a devious one, that Mr Tripton, and Master Daffyd had a weakness for the gaming table. The Geraints were rich enough then but one wild night when Master Daffyd was in his cups he lost a fortune to the Englishman, and couldn't pay what he owed except by land. And that's how it is today, and how it'll be with the present master, your husband, till he's enough gold in his pocket to regain his rights.' She sighed. 'How he'll do it heavens known. But that is the bargain made. So work and stint and scrape we must to go along with him. There was another side to it as well. Something more. Something I'll not be talking about to you – a young bride. Maybe you'll never have to know. Maybe –' Her voice droned to a halt. I tried to probe more out of her, but she refused to talk.

An hour later Owain returned.

He strode into the kitchen wearing high boots, a stove hat and his cape from which water was dripping. After a swift glance at Mrs Maddox he handed the latter to the housekeeper and as she took them to an adjoining small drying room, he flung himself into a heavy spindle-backed chair, stretched a leg out, and remarked shortly, 'You can help. Here –' indicating the boot, 'give a tug, girl. You're not yet too weak to offer a hand, I hope?'

Taken aback by his sharpness I knelt down as any servant might do, aware of the glowering look on me, and half forced the boot from his leg. Irritably he pushed me away then, and ended the process himself.

'Oh, get up,' he growled. 'And don't look so bewildered, for God's sake.'

I straightened up trying to curb a hot rush of anger and humiliation; luckily, perhaps, Mrs Maddox returned the next moment and started fussing round him with brandy and hot water, and soothing servile words to dispel his dark mood. Clearly the business, whatever it was, had not gone well with him in Abergavenny. During the meal that followed he hardly spoke. His expression remained sullen under the thatch of black hair which had curled crisply from the rain about his head and sideburns. Did he ever smile? I wondered, or was it always to be like this, a life without joy, youth, or a chance of laughter?

'It's not fair – not *fair*,' I protested to myself that night when I went alone to bed. 'I didn't *want* this marriage, or to be marooned in this dark forbidding house.' Not even the baby that was developing in my womb. I had only wanted one person in my life, and that was Bryn. And Bryn had deserted me.

Tears of emotion rose from my throat to my eyes. But they didn't fall. I stifled them as in future I decided to stifle all haunting longings to be back in Nanty-Clyd, of 'Polly the Post's' friendly face and the singing from inn and church. Oh, it was terrible to have such frustrated passions in me, such wild tumult in my heart that suddenly it made me want to die. Yes, just for a moment or two when I stared out on the dark lonely night and heard only the sad soughing of wind and rain about the window I would have welcomed death – to have lain and drowned in the rushing stream tumbling through the dark trees sweeping me to eternal forgetfulness. But the vision was too brief to be true.

Life. I must live, for the child's sake, if not my own.

Then I remembered. Remembered what Owain Geraint had said about the baby being sent away. Something changed in me from that moment. It should not be. If the child went, so would I. Somewhere, somehow. In the meantime I would endure as stoically as possible the course before me. With Mrs Maddox's help it might not be too bad.

At least I was spared the physical attentions and proximity of Owain Geraint.

So the days passed through summer towards autumn; days in which I learned to churn butter, ride horseback, see meals were satisfactory yet frugally prepared, give a hand on the land, if required, even potato gathering, when only two months' from my time. On occasion I was expected to make a brief appearance when visiting farmers from Usk way appeared, or possibly a business acquaintance having something to do with mining. At such times I was careful to wear a full crinoline gown, carefully designed to disguise as adequately as possible my figure, for which Owain had grudgingly allowed me to purchase the material. Mrs Maddox had made it up – she was a competent needle-woman. It was of a heavy brown silk, modestly high-necked, and dull I thought. But my husband had already professed a dislike of frills and fallals, and as there was no-one except the housekeeper and farm workers, Owain and his rare male visitors to see, it didn't really matter. His only comments before introduction to any of his cronies were for me to behave quietly and be as inconspicuous as possible.

'No one will care whether you're with child or not,' he said once. 'It's business we'll be embroiled with.'

The 'business', I learned later, was with coal. Owain had

once owned large shares in a mine near Newport, most of which had had to be sold when Llangarrack fell on hard times. This was another cause of the endless routine of work, work, work, overshadowing the atmosphere of the house. He meant somehow to be able to invest again. Oh, what a joyless business it was.

Miraculously, though, I managed to find rare moments to take a short wander up the narrow lane leading between the higher domes of the dark bluish-shadowed mountains. They were very beautiful that autumn. The small white star-shaped flowers of the wild strawberries had gone, but a few berries still peeped from the undergrowth along the valley. The smell of brown bracken, heather, and fallen leaves from the windblown trees were sweet and heady in the air. Under different circumstances, I could have been happy there. But the future held no satisfaction for me.

Only a gnawing fear.

Sometimes, very rarely, I managed to dispel its hovering cloud from my mind – intervals when I was consciously aware only of the mellow haze of autumn sunlight dappling the clustered yellow and brown of woodlands to fiery misted gold. The narrow valley then became a mysterious magic pathway leading to an enchanted world, free of the domestic and physical chains that bound me to Llangarrack.

Once, before the weight of my own body held me back, I walked further than usual, and took a winding narrow path up a slope of the ridge where three counties were said to meet. I'd only climbed a short distance of the mountain, having passed a small farmstead, a shepherd's hut, probably on Llangarrack land, on the way. Further on, partly hidden by a copse of stunted bushes and trees there emerged a small building looking like a miniature derelict castle, that could have been in the past, I supposed, a hunting lodge or watch tower. I was no historian, of course, but I had read of legendary Welsh fables in books borrowed from Nanty-Clyd library, and instantly my imagination was stirred.

A narrow path tangled by briars and obstructing undergrowth led to its entrance which was tangled by ivy and weeds, but accessible, looming eerily dark beyond the broken arch of a doorway. I pushed my way through and found myself in a very small interior festooned with cobwebs, and thick underfoot with moss protruding between granite slabs. A beam of light filtered from the opposite wall, coming, I saw with some astonishment, from, a further door slightly ajar. Unable to curb curiosity, I went in.

What a difference.

Here was no dark hole of a cavern, but a snug small place with stone walls carefully patched and cemented from the elements. In one quarter was a mass of dry sweet hay, indented as though someone had recently lain there. A dozen steps, perhaps more, curved upwards to the stone ceiling, where, from the light of a small Gothic-styled window, a trap-door was discernible which opened, presumably to the sky.

Wild thoughts of mystery and adventure chased through my brain. Although empty, desolate, and partly ruined, the small tower held an uncanny sense of life. Someone had been there recently, obviously. A glass goblet lay in one corner by the hay, and a small piece of linen, as though from a cuff or perhaps a handkerchief, lay on the bottom step. And did a faint smell of expensive perfume tinge the atmosphere? But no. *No*, commonsense told me, that could not be. What I smelled must be the lingering odours of late summer, of heather, and the last wild flowering of nature.

I would have liked to stay and explore longer, but the fear of Owain's wrath if he discovered I'd been away from work on my own drove me away. Picking up my skirts above my boots I left hurriedly, turning only once for a brief quick glance at the miniature tower. The light of a fading sun struck sideways across the stone front, and I noticed what before had not been visible – a curious emblem, or coat of arms perhaps – carved above the entrance. I couldn't, nor had I time, to decipher the inscription, but fancied the shape of a large crow, was intertwined with an intricate pattern of crossed swords and leaves.

The light was fading rapidly.

I was suddenly afraid.

When I reached Llangarrack, Owain was in the kitchen waiting for me.

'Where have you been?' he asked coldly. 'You know very well I wanted the meal early tonight. Or had you forgotten?'

'Yes, perhaps I had,' I answered recklessly. 'I'd been working hard all day. Why shouldn't I have a breath of air and a few minutes on my own occasionally?'

'It's not for you to ask questions,' came the curt reply. 'And I'll have none of your insolence. Be careful, Miss. If you weren't in the sad despicable condition you are I'd treat you as the wilful baggage you are and put you over my knee.' He paused before continuing in lower tones. 'So just you remember, and ask my permission in future before you take yourself off rambling the countryside.'

I said nothing, but bit my lip and thought, 'And some day you'll discover I'm not here any more to be bullied and threatened. Yes, that's what you'll find out, and it won't be so long either.'

With which decision forming hot and strong in me, I lifted my head, and marching haughtily in front of him, from the kitchen, down the hall, and up to the bedroom.

IV

During the next two months Owain's mood unpredictably changed.

'No need for you to be on your feet all day now,' he said one afternoon. 'Don't want you having an accident or being ill. That would be bothersome to Mrs Maddox. So take things easy. As long as you don't go wandering up the valley I shan't grumble. Time to get into a proper routine when the birth's over and done with.'

Inwardly I winced, knowing that his cold impersonal remark referred to the day he could be rid of the infant I carried. Curiously, it was not the child's welfare that so initially concerned me any more, but a determination to keep what was mine. Owain had had my dowry, and no doubt when the opportune moment arose he'd claim my body. But the baby was my own very special property, a part of *me* and this he should not have. I forcefully subdued any memory of Bryn; all the love I'd once had for him had receded into a dark cloud of resentment and painful hostility. Indeed the idea of having to subjugate myself to any man now, was offensive, and if possible I would somehow escape the union with the dark-browed stranger forced on me by my unknown impersonal guardians. During my first days at Llangarrack I'd contemplated running away, but instinct had told me that in the condition I was, I'd soon have been caught and brought back to face hard consequences.

Later, after the child was born, I'd be fit surely, and capable somehow of getting us both safely off together – to the valleys, maybe, and eventually Newport where I was unknown and might find some job. Or perhaps Polly the Post would help. If I could reach Nanty-Clyd at night unseen and unrecognised, she would take me in. I was sure of it. And she had friends in Newport and a sister, a farmer's wife, near Usk. Life at Llangarrack had already shown I had a certain aptitude for dairy work.

Oh, yes. It was possible.

And also only a dream as yet.

But I couldn't think further.

And so the mornings and nights went by, one by one, while the leaves on the trees turned from yellow to brown and gradually fell like tired butterflies to the ground leaving the branches lean and dark against leaden skies.

One morning I had a surprise which was really quite a shock.

'I have guests coming tonight,' Owain said, 'and I shall expect you to attend at dinner. I was informed by the Widow Price that you had learned a modicum of social manners, so you'll kindly dress for the part. Put on as much of a show as you can, smarten yourself – here –' he flung a packet on the kitchen table, ' – take it upstairs, try it on and see if it fits. If it doesn't, if there's any letting out to do –' he smiled wrily – 'you'd better get on with the business. I bought this the other day for just such an occasion as tonight. And don't stare. Take that half-wit look off your face, and put the frillies on.'

I flushed.

'There's no need to be so rude. And if I don't choose to act like any – any –'

'Whore?' he broke in, and his smile became bitter. 'But that's what you are, isn't it? A devious, scheming little madam palmed off on me carrying something I never wanted or knew about.'

'But you had my dowry.'

He gave a short unpleasant laugh. '*And* more besides,

don't forget. So if you value your skin, madam, get out of my sight and don't appear again until I see you bright and splendid in the hall waiting to receive my guests.'

'Me? As I am?'

'Don't worry about your shape. I'm known to be a very virile fellow.'

Luckily at that moment Dilly entered the kitchen. Owain turned on his heel, muttered something under his breath, pushed the girl aside and left the kitchen by the side door, and the next moment could be seen striding past the window on his way to the stables.

Dilly gave me a sidelong curious glance, but I said nothing, just picked up the parcel and with my head high hurried through the entrance to the hall and up the stairs with the box under my arm.

I opened it in the bedroom, hands still trembling from anger and fierce hurt pride. How dare he speak to me like that? How *dare* he? Tears of wild confused emotion churned in my breast gathering in a thick tight knot at my throat.

Then – *then* I saw the gown.

It was of rich red satin, hooped from the waist, with very full wide skirts panelled on both sides. Its hem was scalloped, bordered in silver-grey ribboned lace. The bodice was low cut at the neck, also lace-edged and the sleeves were embroidered at the wrists with similar ribbon.

To say I was astonished is an understatement; the dress must have been extremely expensive, and its flamboyance seemed completely uncharacteristic of Owain's taste. For me, too.

But why? *Why*? When up till then, ever since our unfulfilled mockery of a marriage he had been so parsimonious? Who were these important people for whom I was requested to put on so colourful a part?

Later Mrs Maddox told me. The *Triptons*! The family Owain was supposed to resent from the great mansion over the mountain. The usurpers of his land and Geraint property.

I could not understand, and told the housekeeper so.

'Maybe you will though,' she said, 'one day. Maybe not. It all depends. In the meantime, my dear, I should try and oblige the master this evening, and look your very best.'

'How can I? As I am.'

She gave me a wise reflective glance. 'Many women have a glow about them when they're carrying,' she told me sagely. 'And you've one, whether you care to believe it or no. Yes, indeed. With a little care you could be quite a beauty in your own wild sweet way of looks.'

All right, I thought defiantly. *All right*! I'd make myself as spectacular as possible, rub my cheeks rosy with geranium petals which were still flowering in the dusty conservatory, dress my dark curls high, threaded with a piece of crimson ribbon once given to me by Bryn, and stand tall, with my chin raised, ready to lift my hand graciously in welcome to the greedy proud pair when they arrived. I practised how I would move and speak, several times before the mirror. The result, I thought, was truly effective for a sixteen-year-old girl. I looked quite twenty or twenty-five, and – a little bold perhaps? – but then Owain must have known the red dress would be startling. My figure? I certainly looked plump. But under the mass of frills and hoops no one could know for *certain* I was with child. Unless they poked me, of course. And I hardly thought they'd do that.

I didn't go downstairs until the sound of horses hooves coming to a halt echoed from the drive. I waited a minute, and then descended. Mrs Maddox was ahead, at the door and Owain, attired in velvet jacket, neckscarf, and fitting twill breeches, dressed smartly as I'd never seen him before and looking quite handsome, was coming out of the library. He glanced up as I reached the last few stairs, and his expression was startled, even a little shocked, certainly not entirely pleased. Well, what *had* he expected?

The door opened. I had a glimpse of horses being led away to the stables, and realised I should certainly be 'one on my own'. For the couple entering were wearing riding kit. Why hadn't Owain prepared me? Why hadn't he told me Master and Madam Tripton would make the journey on horseback? I had another far more suitable gown in blue velvet made by Mrs Maddox that would have shown better taste for the occasion. The red dress was wrong – quite wrong. Surely Owain must have known?

However, I pulled myself together with an effort, and went forward, hand extended as I'd planned, although my heart was beating painfully.

Through the soft gleam of lamplight her beauty was striking – fair hair so pale it appeared almost silver-white above the rich olive-green jacket. And the suit was no ordinary riding costume; the full velvet skirt was embroidered at the hem, the jacket was shaped to accentuate an abnormally small waist and likewise delicately stitched and patterned at the cuffs. Behind her shoulders a cape flowed in graceful folds. Everything about her was exquisite, from the silky plumes of her intriguing boat-shaped hat perched saucily above the delicately featured countenance to the elegant pointed toes of her boots.

She was indeed like an image from a fairy tale stepping graciously for a privileged period into the real world. Beside her I felt clumsy, awkward, and somehow garish. Her manners, too, were perfect, although I sensed behind the sweet smile an unknown quality that could mean anything, genuine pleasure at meeting me, or something very different – a certain supercilious derision which seemed to flood her azure eyes briefly with amused contempt. It could have been my imagination, of course. But the conviction remained with me that despite her perfect manners she resented my being there.

Her husband was very different – considerably older, quite ten years Owain's senior, I guessed, bluff and hearty-looking, also richly clad, and with a hard handshake that made me wince. I could feel his eyes travelling from the top of my dark curls to the tips of my toes peeping under the scalloped hem of my red gown as though assessing some lusty young brood mare. They were very small, shrewd eyes, and I knew from the twitch of his rather sensuous lips above the heavy chin that 'my condition' was quite obvious. It was obvious also that he adored his wife and was still dazzled by her glamour.

The whole occasion of meeting and dining with this affluent couple – supposedly so resented by Owain – proved an altogether bewildering experience. To begin with my husband appeared to be a completely different character from the one I'd grown to know during day to day life. He behaved extremely courteously to everyone present, even myself whom he treated as an equal with chivalrous respect, addressing me as 'my dear', and 'my love', and alluding to me when addressing the Triptons as his young wife who was in 'a somewhat delicate condition of health'.

I could not understand it.

They were the people I'd been led to think of as his enemies and plunderers of his land. Yet his smiles and manners, over the wine, were gracious, implying a cordiality I was sure, in my own mind, wasn't genuine. Once or twice I caught his dark eyes turned sharply on Eleanor Tripton, and the expression in them was unfathomable. Then quickly it changed again, and he was all superficial praise and compliments.

As time wore on I began to feel the evening a strain. I wasn't used to small talk and Madam had a curious knack of making me feel, and doubtless appear, countrified, and a nobody, although her words never failed to retain their sugary sweetness. Although she made flattering allusions to my attire, I knew that in comparison with herself I must look slightly garish and over-dressed. Beneath the exotic red silk my skin felt hot and damp. But it was obvious she was completely at ease giving the impression of water-lily coolness. The cream blouse above the olive green skirt was styled simply, with just a suggestion of lace at the base of her slender throat, her wonderful hair drawn away from the temples to reveal the fine bone structure of her face. Candlelight accentuated flattering shadows of her jaw. Oh, yes; she was a beauty, and one of fine taste obviously skilled in the art of subtle make-up.

Her voice, too, had a clear, flute-like quality, which through its very gentility was arresting. I did my best to match my English to hers – but couldn't help being aware of its lilting Welsh quality. Sometimes a phrase or colloquialism reminiscent of Nanty-Clyd slipped off my tongue before I was aware of it. Then I caught Owain's glance sharply upon me. Whether in approval or the reverse I didn't know. There was no flicker of expression on his face. As always, when his attention was forced my way he appeared hard and withdrawn without any real feeling or interest.

The meal seemed endless. However Mrs Maddox had concocted such a lengthy and intricate dinner I didn't know, especially as the only help she'd had on this occasion was Dilly's assistance. She must be tired, I thought, but perhaps not. Perhaps there'd been stimulus for her in being given the chance of demonstrating once more her art of providing a spread for 'gentry'. And there was certainly no sign of stinting, concerning the expense. I knew nothing of wines, and my only experience of spirits was the advantage of keeping a small bottle of brandy stored away in a safe spot, as it had been at the Widow Price's – in case of an emergency or illness. But I sensed instinctively that the liquor provided for the Triptons was the very best.

Somehow the meal drew to an end. Master Tripton and my husband retired to the study for a chat and smoke and I was left to entertain the lovely guest in the best parlour where a log fired burned, and everything had been cleaned and polished – dust sheets removed, and tables and chairs waxed to reveal, despite a certain wear and tear of age, something of former glory.

The interview, to me, was a nerve-racked bore. How we even started to converse, I can't remember. But I do recall that sweet cultured voice murmuring, following a few meaningless rejoinders, 'How refreshing it will be to think of this old place echoing with the patter of tiny footsteps.' The heat of my body rose; my skin burned.

'I suppose so,' I said automatically, 'but that – that won't be for some time yet.'

'Not very long, surely, my dear? Oh, don't blush. I'm *pleased* for you, and for – Owain.' Was it my fancy or did her tones sharpen just a little. 'He'll be so proud.'

'I hope so.'

'But aren't you certain? He's always so wanted a son.'

'Have you any children?' I asked suddenly, bluntly, determined to break her sly questioning.

The faint smile left her lips. The lovely azure eyes narrowed perceptibly.

'No. To the mutual regret of both my husband and myself. But on the other hand – perhaps it's as well. We lead a very busy existence, and my husband travels a great deal. Sometimes I accompany him, sometimes not. It all depends. Frequently I think it would be nice to have a young life to fuss over and spoil. On the other hand children *can* be a frightful tie.' She sighed. 'Maybe I'm not the maternal kind. But you obviously are.' Her supercilious glance, the faint contempt as she studied my ballooning crinoline, sparked off my hot temper.

'Thank you,' I retorted sharply. 'I realise I'm not looking my best. But – but – there's no need to –'

'My dear, my dear,' she interrupted soothingly, in mock concern. '*Please* don't be upset; don't take me wrongly. The last thing I wish to do is to hurt your feelings in any way. And believe me you *look charming*, so pretty and young, and cosy. I only hope Owain appreciates you as a caring husband should, and that you're happy. Are you?'

The abrupt question took me off my guard.

'I *try* to be,' I answered honestly.

'*Try?*' She gave the tinkle of a laugh. 'What an extremely odd confession for a young bride.'

'I don't think so,' I said with a sudden spurt of confidence. 'When everything's so different there's bound to be some sort of adjustment. And that means, well, making an effort sometimes. Don't you agree?'

She studied me thoughtfully for a moment, then conceded, 'Of course. *Naturally*. And life at Llangarrack must indeed be a *very* great change for you from – where is it you come from, my dear?'

'Nanty-Clyd,' I told her with a defiant thrust of my chin.

'Ah, yes! That's a small town, isn't it, Welsh mining, I believe. One of the industrialised valleys?'

'There are mountains, too,' I said, remembering, painfully, one of them, and adding childishly, 'and lots and lots of tiny blue butterflies in the summer. Wild pansies, too. And –' I broke off, realising perhaps I must sound very naive and foolish.

'How sweet!' came the crypt remark. 'Do go on. I love to hear about other places and how the poor live.'

'*Poor?*' my voice sounded shrill in my own ears. 'Not everyone's *poor* there. The valley people are very proud and work hard to get a decent living. Of course, when a mine closes there's hardship sometimes. And anyway, I don't see there's anything to be despised in not having much money.'

'You're *hurt!*' Her voice held assumed surprise and a kind of pitying condescension. 'There was nothing personal in my remarks, Olwen. You don't mind me calling you Olwen, I hope? I was simply referring to existence en masse.'

'There couldn't be, could there?' I said. 'Anything personal, I mean. If you *must* know, Mrs Tripton, when my husband and I were married I had a proper dowry.'

Her smile was unpleasantly suggestive.

'So I – understand.'

'What do you mean? If you're suggesting –'

'My dear girl, I'm suggesting nothing. It was always understood that when a suitable wife could be found for Owain the deal would be settled. I know a very great deal about Geraint affairs. We're very old friends, you see. On both sides. That's why I was a little curious concerning your background.'

'So am I –' I could have said. But with my imagination working quickly I remarked, 'My father and mother are dead. I was brought up under the care of guardians. My family was a very old one. We had a crest and a title, I think – I'm not sure. Perhaps – perhaps if you're so interested you should ask my husband.'

She was obviously nettled.

'Indeed yes. That is quite an idea.'

I smiled as sweetly as possible. After a moment she dropped the play-acting continuing acidly, 'You have quite a quick little mind behind your innocent exterior, haven't you? But a word of advice: don't be *too* sure of your position here. I *know* Owain. You don't, yet. Believe me, he's fanatical in pursuing what he wants. So long as you're of use your position as his wife may be secure. But if you fail –' she shrugged her elegant shoulders, ' – I wouldn't be in your shoes for anything in the world.' Her gorgeous eyes opened wide upon me, limpid dark-fringed eyes holding the changing light of moorland pools, almost hypnotic. 'And never say I didn't warn you, Olwen. You see Owain and I were once more to each other than you will ever know.'

I stared at her dumbly for a second before saying, 'Oh. I see. Well, that's no affair of mine.'

'No. And I advise you to keep things that way.'

'I shan't mention it, if that's what you mean.'

She shrugged again.

'For *you* it would probably be wiser not. But as for me, I really don't care.'

At that precise moment the sound of men's voices and footsteps sounded from the hall.

Eleanor Tripton got up from the chair, and drew an elegant hand over one temple where a curl had strayed.

'Here they come, our precious men.' She flung me a sly glance. 'You look slightly hot. May I offer you cologne from my reticule?'

'No, thank you,' I replied shortly, almost adding, 'I want nothing from you', but managing to curb any show of rudeness on my part.

The next minute the door opened, and Henry Tripton entered, followed by Owain.

V

The dinner party with the Triptons was the last occasion before the baby's birth that Owain appeared to take any particular notice of my presence in his house. We met occasionally at meals in the kitchen, but whenever possible it was obvious he chose to avoid me and took his repast elsewhere – either in his study, on his rounds of the estate – sometimes in the groom's rooms by the stables, at variable hours.

Winter weather came suddenly that year with icy winds sweeping down the valley followed by flurries of snow that became steadily heavier shrouding the mountains and hill-folds, taking the narrow paths and lanes of the vicinity into a thick carpet of white. Only glimpses of the darker branches of the trees could be seen, and the rare visits I had once made to the small hamlet of Skorren were completely curtailed.

Except for Mrs Maddox and Dilly I felt completely alone. Under the normal circumstances subtle movements of the new life within my body would have given comfort and an incentive for the future; but as my time drew near a curious depression settled on me. I felt tired and chilled by the lack of love around me. The housekeeper was kind, it was true. But I couldn't help sensing that beneath her outward solicitude lay a certain condemnation. She had known early, of course, she must have done, that the child wasn't her master's, and although she forebore from any deliberate questioning leading remarks of hers, at times, had indicated curiosity – a curiosity I'd always outwardly ignored and failed to satisfy by one word.

More than once she'd remarked, 'When you give the master his own son, things will be well between you.' And I'd known she was not referring to the baby I carried, but to the child yet to be conceived.

I tried not to think of that. The very idea of any inevitable intimacy with Owain Geraint filled me with increasing apprehension. Very occasionally, when I was least expecting it, I caught a look in his narrow dark eyes, speculative and calculating under heavy lids, that told me in this one thing he would have his way. Love me or want me he might not; but he meant to claim my body and beget his son. My days of comparative physical freedom were swiftly drawing to a close.

Two months, he'd said. After two months – my spine stiffened and pulses trembled – a sick, strange feeling flooded me as I imagined his strong hands about me, his manhood hard in my flesh, not as Bryn had been, but without mercy or tenderness.

Escape. Would it be possible?

I'd contemplated the idea so often, knowing it would be difficult and probably impracticable. Polly the Post, after all, might not welcome me, and even if I reached Nanty-Clyd the Widow Price would see to it that I was either sent back to Llangarrack immediately or put in charge of the detestable authorities again, even the police. Bryn might *just* help if he saw me with his own child in my arms. But I didn't really think so, because I didn't believe in him any more.

And anyway, I told myself stubbornly, I'd no intention of pushing myself upon folk who didn't want me. I was proud still. Better to stick my present existence than humbling myself to be treated as any vagabond thieving tinker.

Providing, of course, that Owain Geraint could be persuaded to keep the baby.

Could he? I didn't know. Perhaps that threat of his to send the child away had been spoken at random through anger at being so deceived.

Yes, I *had* deceived him. And although hard and domineering there'd been moments recently when his voice and expressions had softened temporarily.

One day, when I'd almost fainted in the kitchen and no one else was around, he'd given me some stimulant or other, made me rest in a chair with a cushion at my back, and said, 'The sooner you're rid of that little bastard you're carrying the better. A silly chit you were to get yourself into such a state at sixteen. That's right, isn't it? You *are* only sixteen?'

I nodded, mutely.

'Well, let's hope it hasn't spoiled you for the future. Carrying a great weight around like that! If it was mine I'd think differently, I suppose –'

'Oh, Mr Geraint – Owain –' I broke off miserably.

'Forget it,' he said gruffly. 'You'll be fine, and well able to give me a string of sons of my own when the time comes. Just take care now. Rest up a bit more and feed well. You were picking at your food yesterday. That's no good. You'll need all the strength you've got for the birth. Now take heed of what I say. I'm not a man to waste words.'

I knew that already. I suppppose everyone did around Llangarrack. He was a man dedicated to one purpose – getting his own back on the Triptons and recovering lost land and rights to the estate. He neither conversed much nor tried outwardly to please any of those who worked for him. Yet he was just; the men and stable boy respected him, and I knew Dilly had a sneaking fondness for his dark looks and stern manner. If his glance chanced to come her way there was a lighting of her eyes that made her briefly almost comely. Yet I knew he really hardly saw her. All that mattered to him, except having an heir, I told myself frequently, were those of acres of moors and grassland, the undulating rich hollows of the mountains and misted summits that seemed to hold a mystic quality for him – something in my good moments I could well understand.

In November before the sudden frosts, the red, brown and gold of fallen leaves scattered the valley lanes and footpaths; grey mists silvered the mornings and evenings, and the pungent scent of rotting undergrowth, ripe fallen fruit and woodsmoke filled the air. In the tiny Methodist Chapel of the hamlet farmers and their families gathered for harvest festival. Oh, it was rich there then. If things had been different with Owain and myself, life indeed could have held a sense of fulfilment. I might even have grown to like him well, and more than that. For propinquity can do much to bring a man and woman close, with the doubts and grudges swept away.

But he had given me no chance, no chance at all.

My child was born during the first week of the snow, and with little discomfort except for the birth pangs of any young mother.

A girl.

She was small, delicately formed, lily-pale, unlike most newly born infants and with eyes luminous and bright as mountain pools. Bryn's eyes. A tuft of silken baby down clung to the damp tiny head indicating that she would probably be fair-haired later. She gave one frail cry after birth, and then lay still and quiet in my arms staring up at me.

From that moment I loved her, and knew I could never give her up. She was part of me, something precious salvaged from the torn emotions kindled by Bryn. Yet I recognised and accepted from the very first, that she was also an entity herself, possessing a unique quality that as the days passed became more evident. She showed none of the tantrums most growing infants had; there was a curious acquiescence about her that puzzled me. With her innocent gaze and rare sweet smile she could have been a fairylike innocent creature from some other world – a child of earth and air, snow-capped mountains, and secret moorland pools.

Different.

Yes, that was the word: 'different'.

Whether Owain noticed any peculiarity about the little girl during those earliest days, I didn't know. Probably not. It was doubtful if he noticed me at all at that time, except as an unwelcome uncumbrance in his household, of no use as a wife either for work, or in bed.

For the first weeks of the child's life he made a point of keeping deliberately out of sight of both mother and daughter. But on the rare occasions when his gaze chanced to fall my way I fancied a calculating wary glance in his eyes that told me the time was near when he would demand the rights of a husband. A *husband*! I'd thought then, almost with derision. A man I hardly knew and who had no interest at all in me save for what I'd brought him in dowry, and the assistance I could give in helping run the place a mite more economically, with the promise of a son ahead.

Oh, I need have no illusions about Owain Geraint. A hard man he was, I'd emphasised to myself many times when a faint feeling of softness for him had threatened. It was folly to have any hopes that time and familiarity might change him. As for the baby, a bargain to him was a bargain. When he thought fit he'd see my tiny daughter was packed off to the foster-parents he'd arranged for, and then that very night, no doubt, come purposefully to the bedroom to rape me. Yes – that's what it would be – married to him or not – it would be rape! For how could any woman worth her salt go willingly to a man ruthless enough to tear a mother and her babe apart? Especially such an innocent gentle little creature as my own tiny Merionne. That's what I called her, Merionne, she was so

small and white and butterfly fragile. Sometimes I would
croon to her a Welsh lullaby I had learned as a child, and
once, hearing me as I sat by the stove in the kitchen, Mrs
Maddox said, 'So that's what you're going to call her, is it?
Merionne? – known as Fair Maid about these parts.'

'Why not?'

'Don't let the master hear you talking so sentiment-
sweet,' the housekeeper said warningly. 'Plain Ann would
be better, and anyway, my dear, the time's coming as you
well know, when she'll be going to her new home. Oh, I
know all about it – I have to, don't I? Seeing as I'm still *part*
mistress of this house.'

Anger rose in me in a great fire of resentment. 'I don't –
I won't – she's *my* child, and if *she* goes, I –'

'No, now. Don't be foolish. You've borne the babe, and I
can understand, indeed so, indeed I can, how your heart
aches at the thought of losing her. But think of it this way.
She'll be better off where she's going. The master's not a
cruel man, a realist, yes, and that's as well, so it is. The folk
he's found for her will be good people, you can take my
word for it, and she'll be brought up in a sensible home to
learn the rights and wrongs of living. I know; believe me, I
know.'

'Like I was to the Widow Price,' I broke in rebelliously,
'without my mam or father, then married off to some
greedy stranger –'

'Hush, hush. It's wild you sound when you speak like
that.'

'Yes, wild. And so is this place and these mountains, and
the wind tearing through the trees. So is my heart. So am
I. There are times when I want to fling myself into the
great rushing stream below, and without Merionne –' I
broke off as sobs half-choked my throat and tears fell
unashamedly from my eyes, catching the tuft of the baby's
small head cradled against my breast.

Mrs Maddox got to her feet, patted my shoulder, and

said with soothing commonsense, 'Cry, mistress, if you must. It's a way of healing, while I get a cup of hot drink for us both.'

She moved away, and presently something of my anguish eased.

That same night after I'd gone to bed and was standing looking down on the cradle where Merionne lay sleeping, one tiny fist curled aainst her bud of a mouth, there was a knock on the door, and Owain came in.

The expression on his face was dimmed in the fitful glow of the small oil lamp, but I sensed something purposeful about him that tensed my nerves to rigid expectancy, and a dread that after the first moment, started a wild beating of my heart.

I waited until he said, 'So you're not yet abed? That's good, I'd no mind to spoil your sleep.'

'I'm a little later than usual,' I remarked.

'Which is as well.' He paused before continuing wrily, 'I may sit, I suppose, on my own bed?'

Drawing my wrap closer about me I answered, 'Of course.'

He seated himself on the quilt, stared at me for some seconds, then resumed, 'Come here, Olwen, I shan't eat you. But the time has come now for us to talk, as you must well know.'

'Talk?' I queried feebly.

A wry smile touched his taut lips.

'As a preliminary.'

'I don't –'

'Did you hear what I said just now? *Come here.*' His voice had hardened.

With an attempt I shrugged, obeyed, and perched straightbacked on the bed beside him, staring straight ahead.

He sprang up impatiently, took a stride or two forwards then back, and stood towering over me, staring down.

'It seems to me,' he said then, 'that it's high time we had the situation clear. You have already spent longer than was arranged for with that little –' there was a brief pause while I waited for the word 'bastard' to be thrown at me. But evidently he thought better of it for he concluded ' – that little offspring of yours. She's being spoiled and doted on too much, and when we married it was not to have a wife lazing most of her days away on an unwanted weakling brat –'

'She's no brat,' I cried jumping to my feet defiantly. 'And she's not unwanted. She's –'

'By me she is; as you well know. On Thursday, therefore, I've arranged for her to be taken to Abergavenny, where her new parents will be waiting to collect her. I can assure you they are respectable folk who will give her a good home. Their name you will never know or her future whereabouts. You'll miss her, at first, I realise that –' His eyes left mine temporarily. 'But there's no point in pleading with me, and if you're wise you'll spare any soft-soap tears on me. I'm a man of my word, and expect you to behave over this matter in an honourable and dignified manner –'

'*Honour?*' The word burst from me wildly. 'What has *honour* to do with it? She's *mine*. I love her. It was *you* who made the cruel conditions –'

'Only when I knew the trick played on me and then it was too late for anything else,' he interrupted harshly. 'If you or the Widow Price had given an inkling of what lay under that prim exterior of yours I doubt if there'd have been any bond at all beween us. But then the Widow didn't know, did she? You'd been a clever young madam indeed. Well, for your own good now you'll see to it that your shrewd little brain is turned in other directions, and oblige me by recognising your –'

'Marital duties?' Unfair or not, I was bitterly sarcastic.

'Exactly. And next time let us hope that the fruit of your ripe young body produces a boy. Mine.'

Before I could think of an apt rejoinder he had made an abrupt movement and gone to the door, where he turned and said in unemotional tones, 'Get yourself ready for bed now. I shall be with you presently.'

Then he was gone, without a glance at the sleeping baby, or a softening look in my direction.

I went to the window mechanically, and stared out of the window at the forbidding bleak line of mountains under a cold moonlit sky. Wild thoughts of escape – of taking Merionne and rushing heedlessly into the frosted landscape – to the Tower perhaps, where we could rest before making our way towards Brecon or Talgarth once more filled me in a torment of confused emotion. But I knew it was to no avail. Not yet. It was still only Tuesday. I had the next day to think things out, and the night following to put any possible plan into action. I would do it. I would – I *would*, I promised myself. Merionne and I belonged together and somehow I would manage to keep her.

Meanwhile, jerked suddenly to the present, my rigid body came to life again. I moved to the cradle and touched the child's soft cheek gently. She didn't stir.

'Oh, Merionne, Merionne bach,' I murmured, 'never fear. You are safe. You belong to me.'

She didn't hear, apparently, and would not have understood even if she did; she was too young, and there was something else. By then, although I would not admit it, I already sensed that my little girl would never be as other normal individuals. 'Different' was the word I'd always used in my mind, but that was an understatement. Therefore, she needed all the more a mother's care.

Very slowly I left her undisturbed. And then, apprehensive, but steeling myself to the inevitable, I undressed, washed, and shivering from the cold air, drew my long-sleeved woollen nightgown over my head and climbed into bed, with the sheets drawn close to my chin.

Five minutes or so later the door creaked.

Owain, wearing some sort of loose wrap, came through, and approached on firm, determined steps, while I lay motionless, eyes shut, as though feigning sleep.

I closed both my heart and body against him. But he took me, his hands and voice caressing at first, gradually hardening with ruthless determination the more I resisted.

Did he murmur at first, 'Cariad, oh, Cariad, give a little, just a little, don't fight – soften, woman –'? I do not know. Perhaps it was all imagination, the pleading before force took over. All I clearly remember now is the passion that seared me, ending in pain and wild throbbing of my flesh in culmination. Was it my own moaning I heard? Or the sudden rising of wind round the old house? There is no telling.

I think I cried, 'Go away, I *hate* you' but of that even I cannot now be sure. There was a despair in me beyond words or reason, despair that I had fought and lost, and would be now forever in subjugation to the dark force that was Owain Geraint.

Unless I got away.

I do not even recall how long it was before he left me – alone at last in the great bed. Near to dawn it must have been, and driven by the gale, rain was lashing through the trees beating their branches against the window, in a restless tattoo of sound. Unpredictably the weather had become warmer overnight; the roads would be mushy, I knew, and not easy to travel. But go I must – somehow, somewhere. Not only for Merionne's sake but my own.

I felt abased and ashamed, not merely by Owain's strength, but my woman's weakness that despite my fear and hatred had finally relished that wild spark of willing subjugation that had briefly blotted out all else.

*

When I went down to breakfast in the morning Owain had left for Newport.

'Got business there,' Mrs Maddox told me, with a questioning look in her eyes. 'Not back till nightfall, so he said.'

My nerves relaxed, and it was then I realised how truly exhausted I was. There would be time then to plan carefully and leave that afternoon, probably when the housekeeper was having her snooze by the kitchen fire.

The extreme greyness of the day, half blurred by rain which had now become a thin drizzle, would probably turn to mist later, and be of help.

So assuming an air of uninterest, I managed to eat a decent breakfast, and afterwards went upstairs to plan for the journey ahead.

*

As I'd thought probable, by the afternoon the thin rain had turned to a chill mist, shrouding the winter landscape into grey uniformity when I recklessly set out on my bid for freedom wearing my thick cape and shawl over my head, with the baby warmly wrapped, slung in a blanket close to what warmth I had in my body. I also carried a bundle containing a bottle of milk, and a sufficiency of food, I judged, for the journey up the winding valley track to the hills Brecon way. Safely in my reticule tied round my waist under my skirts was all the money I'd managed to save from Owain's mean household allowance. Not much, but enough to pay for brief shelter and rest, if necessary, when I reached any village or town.

The track wound ribbon-like under the region of Talgarth and there was a good deal of rough climbing to cover before any sign of civilization appeared. I supposed vaguely Crickhowell also must be in the same direction, but places and names meant nothing to me except that any village or town reached must be a further step to the

mining area of Nanty-Clyd, where, I hoped, Polly the Post
would have sympathy for my plight, and take pity on the
tiny scrap of humanity peeping like a frail lily-bud from
her covering.

It was hard walking; the earth now was damp and soggy.
In spite of the thaw, thin drifts of snow still dappled the
scene, trickling in sluggish streams to the narrowing valley.
On either side the rounded dark domes of the mountains
crouched like huge primitive beasts forever seeming to
draw closer in elemental hostility. Yet in the summer they
had been so beautiful.

I recalled the day I'd passed the tower and investigated
its secret interior, the frail suggestion of feminine
perfume, a reminder of human presence lingering there.
Always I'd meant to return; but Owain had forbidden me,
and somehow my interest had died. Neither did it revive
that late afternoon when I passed. To the contrary there
was something menacing about it, a magnetic sense of
impending doom that seemed to whisper through a frail
rising wind: 'Enter here and it will be to your peril.' And to
my mind came one of Keats' poems, 'La belle dame sans
merci hath thee in thrall'.

English literature, but curiously evocative somehow of
the Celtic region I travelled during those wearying hours.

Yes, I became utterly weary. More weary than I
consciously realised; with vagrant half-formed thoughts
echoing through my brain meaninglessly: of the Widow
Price, Bryn, blue butterflies, and singing from far away,
merging into the soughing of wind and gurgling of
flowing water. Yet on I went, impelled by the one blind
instinct to get away and save my child. Occasionally I
stopped to feed her. She was good, and quiet as ever. And
sadness that held an anguish of beauty, temporarily
dispelled other haunting thoughts. But the light was
swiftly darkening, and the time came when I dared no
longer pause, knowing, if I did, that it might be difficult,

perhaps impossible, to get to my feet and continue.

My boots, like weights, seemed to pull me down, as though the hungry sucking earth was eager for sustenance.

'Oh! but what morbid imaginings!' I told myself more than once. 'Pull yourself together, Olwen March. You're alive and strong. You can do it – for the little one, the innocent babe you bore.'

And so we continued, on our way, each step sapping strength and energy, driven by purpose and willpower to survive.

VI

With nightfall the cold mist thickened, and there was no moon to be seen. Merionne, though still held sheltered against me under the damp cloak showed restlessness, something I'd never known before, and from time to time little sounds of unease and a faint wheezing told me she was beginning to feel the cold. My arm ached; my feet became numb. I knew dejectedly that my departure had been rashly planned. I should have risked the chance of being caught and questioned, and taken the opposite route through the hamlet towards Abergavenny where I might perhaps have had a lift in a farmer's cart or with some passing pedlar.

My journey now could only be from instinct, and the incline was steepening. There, somewhere looming either behind or to the east, must be 'Table Mountain'. Or was I quite wrong? I simply could not tell. I was lost. Twice I'd somehow blundered off the narrowing path, turned back, plodding to my left. But in such a swirling miasma of fog it could mistakenly have been to the right. Where, then, was I? There was no known landmark discernible. Nothing but fitful glimpses of shapeless rocks and undergrowth – no welcome glow even of a shepherd's lantern. The silence, except for the constant drip, drip of nature, of squelching bog and moaning wind, was claustrophobic and frightening.

'I'm sorry,' I muttered aloud to the baby. 'Oh, Merionne, I'm sorry –' and a second later the toe of one boot caught a stone, and I fell.

Merionne was half dislodged from my arm, but I still held her as my foot doubled under me in an excruciating stab of pain.

I clutched at a bramble, tore my hand, and tried to rise but couldn't. A bird, disturbed, swooped close to my face, squawking; and instinctively I gave a cry. It was then that the thudding began – a rhythmic thudding almost simultaneous with the terrible thudding of my own heart. I managed to ease myself up a little, waiting, listening. There was a rustling from somewhere above, and looking up I saw the blurred dark shape of a horseman coming to a halt beside me.

'In the name of God –' I heard a familiar voice say as the figure dismounted. 'What are you doing out here? Are you *mad*?'

I didn't answer. Relief too great for words temporarily held me dumb.

He knelt down, drew the shawl aside, and must have glimpsed the tiny face of the baby puckered up with cold and discomfort.

'You little fool,' Owain said to me. 'You silly idiot chit of a woman. Two hours I've been searching. *More*. Ever since I got back to Llangarrack. Come along now. Up with you –'

A strong hand was on my arm, but the first movement made me wince with pain as the world spun with darkness. Only for a second or two. I'd come round the next, and managed to take his support.

He lifted me on to the horse, then picked up the baby and fastened her securely under my cape, placing a rug he'd bought, round both of us. Before we started off he made me sup brandy or whisky – I didn't know the difference – and the return journey to Llangarrack began. Owain led the grey by its bridle; somewhere a night bird squawked shrilly, as though in derision. No word was spoken on the way, the mist neither lightened nor lifted.

The liquor must have helped me. I felt strangely calm, with acceptance at last of the inevitable. In the morning I should have to face not only Owain Geraint's anger, but the departure of Merionne.

My one chance of reaching 'Polly the Post' was gone. Merionne was lost to me.

It didn't occur to me I could be wrong.

*

In the morning, following a brief hour's exhausted sleep and breakfast which I did not want, I was told by Mrs Maddox that Owain wished to see me in his study.

He was standing with his back to the door glaring out of the window over the grey scene outside when I went in. A meagre fire burned in the grate. The air, though chill, smelled stuffy, carrying the damp odour of ancient books and old leather indicating it had been used very little in recent years. He turned, went to the fire, gave it a poke, saying tersely, 'Don't just stand there. Come here and sit down. What I've got to say won't take long.'

I obeyed mutely; he didn't at first look at me, just sat opposite, head thrust forward a little, hands on his knees, staring into the wan flames. Then suddenly he jerked to attention and fixed me with a very straight gaze.

'You were a little fool last night,' he said, in cold level tones, 'but you must know that. I hope you realise also something of the trouble you caused.' He paused, and when I didn't speak, continued, 'But there! I don't intend to lecture. There's no point, is there, since you seem beyond rational behaviour –'

'*Rational?*' I broke in. 'Did you – do you expect me to behave rationally under the circumstances, the wretched conditions forced on me? I know you never wanted Merionne – I didn't myself, particularly, until she was born. But I'm her mother. And all you've thought about these months is getting rid of her. Oh, I know it was arranged. A bargain was made. But you can't hold me to it, because it's inhuman. No one, *no* one has the right to bargain with flesh and blood –' I broke off, breathing quickly, almost gasping, my voice a rasp in my own throat.

'*Stop* it!' He strode towards me, enclosing one shoulder hard. 'For heaven's sake, spare the melodrama. I've no taste for it, or for you either, if you're so determined for neurotic scenes. After the other night I *did* think perhaps we might make a reasonable go of things, despite your show of tantrums. I was even prepared to give second thoughts to my so-called inhuman conditions. Now I'm not so sure.'

Wild hope soared in me. 'You mean ?'

He released me, turned his back on me, and walked to the window once more.

'I mean,' he said at length, not looking at me, 'as it's a girl, and a weakling chit at that, I've no particular desire any more to waste money and valuable time in seeing she's brought up by trustworthy folk. She can remain here provided you see to it that she's kept out of my way and doesn't interfere with your responsibilities at Llangarrack. No simpering and fussing over her. No fallals for dressing her up as a fine lady-to-be. If she's strong enough she'll work when she's grown; in the meantime she'll keep to the kitchen quarters where Dilly or Mrs Maddox can see to her food, and not be around at all when I'm there. Do you understand?'

'Yes,' I said, although only one fact registered, that Merionne was not to be sent away after all, 'and thank you.'

'There's no thanks due for being a fool,' he stated callously. 'If I had any sense I'd send the two of you packing. As it is, see you do your duty now and be ready for me when I'm woman-hungry. So far I've been pretty patient, but I want a son, Olwen. Then maybe one day I'll be able to stick the sight of that little changeling around.'

Following a quick glance at Merionne, he turned and left me. I stared after him, grateful in one way for the concession he'd made, yet hating his harsh words, and despising, with a shiver up my spine, my own weakness in recalling the wild passion between us of only two nights before.

Mrs Maddox, I'm sure, knew more of the relationship between Owain and myself than she admitted. When I was helping her in the kitchen later she said, 'You're lucky, all things considered. Indeed, yes. One day he may even come to think kindly on the poor little thing – providing you're sensible and give him the son he wants.'

'What do you mean by "poor little thing"?' I said fiercely. 'My baby's *beautiful*, and I can't produce a boy at will.'

'Hm. Oh, yes, she's a pretty little creature, I grant you that,' the housekeeper conceded grudgingly, 'but beauty's little good without something in the head, mistress. It's not my place maybe to talk so, but for your own good you should face the truth. There's something not right about her. Never a cry or sound from her – no tantrums or screaming or response when you go near. Nothing but that faraway look and a smile sometimes. At what? There's no telling. So that's why I say you should be grateful to the master. It's my belief he'll get nothing of use from her, ever. Yet he's shouldered the responsibility like the good man he is at heart, knowing it would be difficult indeed to find any decent normal family or couple willing to take such as her into their home.'

A sharp retort was on my lips, but I stifled it, because I knew, without admitting it, that what she said about my tiny daughter was true.

So the weeks and months passed, and summer came – a period during which for the sake of peace I endeavoured to keep the baby and my husband apart. Our love-making – if such it could be called – was intermittent and could give me no lasting pleasure, since I knew that it was a means only for begetting a son, his heir. When that was achieved I should probably be left free to live a nun's life. It was a chilling thought, the more so because I suspected the haughty Mistress Tripton over the mountain still held some attraction for him. What she'd implied at our first meeting of a former attachment between herself and Owain had held some basis. When I'd quizzed Mrs Maddox one day about the matter the old woman had let out the truth quite bluntly.

'There's no harm in your knowing how things were,' she said, 'for the best it is; for you're bound to find out one day. She was pledged to him, you see. Besotted with her he was – well, you have to admit she's a beauty in her own toffee-nosed fashion. Yes, it was all arranged, banns and all –'

'You mean they were to be married?'

'Of *course*. What else? And then that rich high-falutin' Englishman comes along, sees her and grabs the haughty madam for himself from under the master's very nose. Mind you, there didn't have to be much *grabbing*, not where *she* was concerned. A fine house, a wealthy husband to give her all she asked for, money, travel, jewels fit for a queen and all the rest. You wouldn't expect a woman of her kind to refuse all that for the sake of a country squire living on limited means at Llangarrack. So that's how it was. And if you ask me *she's* the one responsible for the dark moods the master goes through sometimes. Behind the drive and the energy, and the stinting and scraping and work, work, *work* – he's remembering. That, and the land. All that was stolen from him has fired a kind of wild revenge. He means to get on top again one day, and prove that the Geraints aren't willing forever to be bested by any jumped-up Englishman. You understand?'

Oh, yes, I understood, looking back recalling Mistress Tripton's words to me, on the evening of the dinner party at Llangarrack, the occasion when she'd told me in her falsely-sweet taunting way how close she and Owain had once been. How gauche I'd felt in the red dress bought for me by my husband! How she must have been despising me in her heart. Had he then intended to humiliate me? Or was it planned as an act of defiance? A genuine jealous wish to parade me before his erstwhile paramour? If the latter he'd made a great mistake. She'd been laughing at me all the time, and at him too, perhaps.

But no. That hadn't been so. A certain look in his narrow eyes, a kindling of their sombre lights, and an answering flash of understanding in her own had betrayed a lingering of the old fascination which I now understood. I should have recognised the situation earlier. Eleanor Tripton and Owain Geraint still hungered for each other. When he'd taken me so violently against my will it had been with no true desire for me as a woman, but through frustration of pent-up longing for his former mistress. Oh, it was humiliating. He had *wed* me yet I had been no more to him than a tool for revenge, and for producing something of himself – a son – to flaunt in her face when the occasion arose.

Well, so far it hadn't happened. Although he'd asserted his marital rights at regular intervals through the warm soft nights of high summer, no child had been conceived, or was likely to be, I thought bitterly. The occasions had been merely acts of physical need without affection or any show of pleasure or tenderness towards me. There'd been no blossoming, no true flowering between us. How then could he expect me to bear his child? Through lust only? Perhaps. It *could* happen, and frequently did, in countless cases where women were forced by their husbands to bear child after child through the years, only to die exhausted and old before their time. It had happened in the valleys; I'd read of it in history books borrowed unknown to Mrs Price from Polly the Post's little library which had told of rich royal households where queens had suffered in the same way.

But I tried to believe this wouldn't be my fate.

I attempted no remedy to stop conception, not knowing any. If I *did* bear Owain's son, I'd do my best to love him, but secretly I had no wish for any child of such a sterile marriage. Yes, sterile indeed it was, I told myself repeatedly during those first months of union with my husband. Everywhere around me nature conceived; young things were born and flourished, flowers starred the hedgerows, trees blossomed, lambs and animals of the fields frollicked. But the heart of the house, Llangarrack itself, brooded in its own bitterness, and following my discovery concerning Owain and Eleanor Tripton I hoped fervently no seed of his would quicken in my womb.

I hated him.

I would pay him out, I would – I *would*! I told myself fiercely more than once. To have married me cold-bloodedly at some sort of bargaining price was bad enough; but to have done so while lusting for another woman was an insult. It didn't occur to me at the time that my wild fit of temper and melodramatic sense of outrage could be caused by something stronger than hurt pride. Jealousy? But why would I be jealous of two people I cared not a jot about, except through being caught in such a miserable trap between them?

Yes. I was caught – trapped.

And very lonely.

Except for tiny Merionne I had nothing and no one in my life to call really my own. And following the first developing months of the baby's life it gradually became apparent to me that she had no feeling for me. Any interest she had was directed towards Owain. On the rare occasions he chanced to pass her lying in her cradle her strange luminous eyes would be upon him, a gurgling sound like that of a young dove cooing would come softly from her throat, and at such times he'd pause briefly, surprised, and perhaps tap her cheek lightly with a finger. He seemed no longer to resent her, and very slowly I became aware of a curious bond forming between the two of them. At the sound of his voice a faint sweet smile would touch her rosebud lips. So she *could hear*. I was grateful for that, though irritated that she took no notice when I spoke her name. Still, she was yet very young. Perhaps, I told myself optimistically, her other senses would develop normally eventually. I would then be able to reason with her, form a rewarding mother-and-daughter relationship.

But no such thing happened. Time passed. At two years old she was unresponsive to everyone but Owain, and far from being annoyed by the situation, he showed signs of being intrigued. Instead of trying to avoid her he took every chance of brief contact – pausing with a smile, when she lifted a small hand to him as he passed. The change in him then, quite startled me. The bitterness left his face giving his stern features a kindly whimisical touch. He appeared years younger, and the smouldering resentment I felt would turn to regret, and a sense of defeat, almost pain, that he could show no gentleness or softening to me, his wife.

It was true that he demanded less labour than formerly from me. All field work was spared me and except for giving a hand in the dairy sometimes, I was expected to conserve my energies for running the house efficiently and seeing that what staff we had put the maximum of energy into their duties. Grudgingly, he'd agreed for another girl to assist Mrs Maddox with the cooking, and an extra man for outside work. So including Dilly, Llangarrack had five regular employees, excluding the extra seasonal workers required at harvesting time and in the spring. Meanwhile, Owain made more frequent visits to Newport. I could sense a fresh determination about him

– a vitality and optimism that suggested he was somehow securing a holding once more in the mining company he'd been forced to abandon.

My instincts proved to be right.

One evening in the early spring of 1863 when I was up later than usual trying to finish stitching a new dress for Merionne, Owain strode into the kitchen, pulled off his stove hat, flung his cape-coat over a chair, and came to the fire where I was seated, not speaking for a moment just staring into the flames with his hands outspread, waiting, as though deep in thought.

I put the sewing down and got up dutifully to attend to his needs, either for ale or broth from the simmering pot. He halted me immediately with a gesture.

'Stop a moment and hear what I have to say. Has Mrs Maddox gone to her bed?'

'Yes. She was ready for it.'

'Good.' He flung me a calculating glance. 'Sit down, Olwen. I've news for you.'

'News?'

'So I said. Some good. Some not so bright.'

My nerves tensed. 'What news, Owain?'

'The good news first, I think. I've managed to recover quite a tidy few of the shares once held by Geraints in the Tyn-Wellan Company. Not enough, mind you, to make us rich, or even comfortable. But it's a beginning, and proof enough to show that frugality pays. Without watching every penny spent I couldn't have done it. So don't get extravagant ideas into your head of wanting this and that, or thinking there'll be any grand changes in our way of life. There won't be – yet. Perhaps in time –' There was speculation in his voice, but his expression remained unchanged. 'The future's unpredictable,' he ended ambiguously.

'Yes.' I didn't know what else to say.

'As for the other matter, you're not going to like it, I'm

afraid. It will be a shock, but I expect you to accept facts without any unnecessary melodrama. All I can say is I'm sorry.' The sudden softening of his tone unnerved me.

'What do you mean? Is it something about Merionne? Have you changed your mind about –'

'Oh, no, no. Nothing to do with the child. There's been tragedy at Nanty-Clyd. Two-thirds of the houses have gone, and more than half the population.'

I stared at him aghast. 'I don't understand. *How*? *What* accident? You're exaggerating. You must be.'

He shook his head.

'There was an explosion at the mine, followed by a landslide made worse by recent heavy rains. A whole chunk of mountain went. Nothing could be done. *Nothing*.'

'But Bryn, and – and –'

'*Bryn?*'

'Bryn's *family* then,' I almost shouted, 'and Polly the Post, the Widow Price –'

'I'm afraid,' Owain replied gruffly, 'you'll not be seeing them again.'

For a moment or two I just stared at him, unable to speak, while cold waves of shock held me rigid. Then I began falteringly, 'you mean –?'

'Taken with the rest,' he stated bluntly. 'And don't look at me like that. I know, I know. It's a sad thing, a terrible thing. But nothing on earth could have prevented it. A freak accident; just one of those unfortunate events that can shatter a whole community. In mining districts –' before he could finish I interrupted:

'The Rhys-Evans, what about *them*? The farm, Marged and Dai, Bryn, Idris, no, *no*. I don't believe it. I *can't* –'

'You *have* to, Olwen.' Owain took me by the shoulders, staring hard into my face, and for a second there was feeling there, a kind of pain I'd never seen before. I shook my head, trying ineffectually to pull myself away.

'I must go,' I cried helplessly. 'I must find out for myself.

They were, they were the only real friends I've ever had. I don't expect you to understand. You *couldn't*. It's impossible –' I babbled on, recalling in that hideous time of shock, quite small unimportant things, stories Bryn had told me of how Marged had had to put an umbrella up on her way to school each morning to ward off a bad-tempered gander they'd had, of the conspiratorial little gleam in Polly the Post's kindly eyes when she pushed a book into my shopping basket that the Widow Price wouldn't have approved of. Oh, so many human incidents that at one time had helped make up my life. Even the Widow Price, stiff and starchy, but true to her convictions always, doing her duty as she thought fit, and having for me under her strict primness a dry kind of affection that had shown itself in a number of small ways. And the miners! the singing! the children! – gone, he'd said, gone.

'I must go,' I insisted again. 'Find out –'

'*No.*' That one word was sharp as the crack of a pistol shot. 'You'll do no such thing. I've checked. All that area of the mountain is devastated. You could do nothing, and find nothing but death, rubble, and mourning everywhere. Now, Olwen, pull yourself together. Thank your stars you're out of it here, with me at Llangarrack. It isn't as though your relationships, any you had, went deep, is it? Except for that Bryn of yours.' Bitterness edged his voice.

'How do *you* know?' I said. 'You've never troubled to find out. You haven't any knowledge at all of what I feel. It isn't *your* worry, Nanty-Clyd wasn't *your* home, you never lived there, or knew the mountain –' I almost choked on the word, remembering the small pansy flowers dotting the short turf, the tiny blue butterflies, and tangy smell of heather and sweet earth when I lay there with Bryn.

'I have no doubt the mountain still remains,' Owain said drily, 'or most of it. The earth itself has a queer knack of survival. Another thing –' he eyed me fiercely – 'don't suggest I've no feelings for the folk who've gone. They were my *people. Welsh.*'

'But more mine,' I nearly said. *Were* they though? Again the old question – who? *What* was I? Where did I come from? What place? What country? Why the mystery? My existence must have had sufficient importance to carry a dowry large enough to tempt a man like Owain Geraint into matrimony. If I'd been a mere nobody, a foundling baby left on some doorstep or at the gates of the orphanage, I would have spent my youth there, working, or even taken to the workhouse itself. But I hadn't been. I'd been given a name 'Olwen March', and trained for marriage to be the wife of a 'gentleman'. In those few fleeting seconds, shocked by tragedy, swift as a lightning flash, the old query of identity sprang to life again, then died as suddenly, while my husband continued:

'Stir yourself. Don't just stand there. There are things to do, girl. You'd better get busy. No use comes from fretting.'

He half raised an arm, and I thought he was going to touch me. But he didn't. He gave a sigh, a little click of his teeth, turned and went to the door where he paused fleetingly to say, 'Why don't you spend a bit of time with Merionne? She seems to see more of Dilly these days than you. A child her age needs the attention of her mother.'

'I'm sure she doesn't miss *me*,' I remarked. '*You're* her god.'

'Oh, don't be ridiculous.'

I smiled. But my heart and eyes were cold. 'It's the truth, Owain. And you know it. I do my best, I've tried quite hard in the past to make warm contact, but there's no response. She behaves as though I wasn't there. Not wilfully, of course. But,' I shrugged, 'she's not normal. And don't say I imagine it. Everyone's noticed.'

'*Everyone?* Farm hands? A simple creature like Dilly? Mrs Maddox? An old woman? You're becoming neurotic.'

The door slammed. He was gone.

Anxiety and depression in me deepened with a strange feeling of abandonment and desolation. I had to face the fact that I wasn't really needed anywhere by anyone. For some time I couldn't foresee any useful or rewarding future. Then, slowly, as commonsense took a hold of my shocked brain I knew what Owain had said was true. My first wild desire to return to Nanty-Clyd immediately and view the tragic scene of destruction would be of no use. One day perhaps, when I was older and more resigned, I might make a visit, recalling hours of happiness once spent there. Threads of memory might then make some pattern and reason for my life. But first of all I had to get the present into order, carve an identity at Llangarrack strong enough to have meaning and a certain power as the wife of Owain Geraint.

It was during those moments of self-knowledge I think that I first realised the tempestuous, transient quality of my wild adolescent hatred of the man I'd married. My hatred had been puerile. An anachronism.

I didn't hate him at all.

During the rare times of passion between us, there'd been a dark hunger kindled that went far beyond conscience or reason. Love wasn't the word. 'Love' belonged to the sentimental youthful world of blue butterflies and Bryn. My feelings for Owain were an instinct and a thirst, holding the wild savage sweetness of mountain streams rushing through windswept trees to the river – of earth and air, and bittersweet scents of storm-drenched earth after rain.

Oh, how foolish I'd been. How naive and gauche and unaware of my own secret self. And how ironic it should take a tragedy such as that of Nanty-Clyd to break the barrier of ignorance.

'Neurotic' Owain had said.

Yes, it was true.

So I had been.

But in future it would be different. Somehow I would make myself indispensable to Owain Geraint, and as *myself*, not merely as a vehicle of bearing his son.

Autumn was a rich, golden one that year, and in spite of uneasy disappointment over my daughter and secret longing to be in loving harmony with Owain – a weakness I did my best to control – the mysterious magic of the shadowed mountain region gradually captured my heart and imagination, becoming a beckoning force that took me on every rare available opportunity up the winding thread of lane curling through mist and sunlight, past the tower towards the high uplands where wild ponies could sometimes be glimpsed galloping in a stream with manes and tails flying, over the furthest ridge.

Generally, in these rambles I walked. But since Merionne's birth I had learned to ride horseback, and very occasionally when Owain was in Cardiff or Newport for the day I had a grey mare saddled and cantered further afield. A mile or so beyond the tower I'd discovered the tumbled remains of what must once have been a small castle or mansion, encircling a deep tarn, fifty yards or so off the main track. I'd dismounted, tethered my horse to a stump of tree, and made my way on foot towards the glistening pool. The water was clear, very translucent, reflecting swimming ever-changing shapes of reeds, deep deep rock and stone ruffled to green, purple, and blue, intermittently washed to sombre grey from passing clouds above.

The effect was mysterious; the more so as the drop to the surface of the water was sheer and shining, clearcut as though a giant sword had been there.

On my return to Llangarrack the first time, I'd mentioned the place to Mrs Maddox. She was instantly on the alert and said reprovingly, 'Oh, you shouldn't have gone there. The master wouldn't have liked it. You stay away in the future, mistress. See that you do.'

'Why?'

'Because it's dangerous. Got a bad name it has. Some say a demon lies there, Y Fall, the dark one himself, always ready for human life. Mind you, I'm a good Methodist, and don't believe in such things. But there's history to it. Indeed there is. Once there was a monastery I've heard, long, long ago, run by a monk that had his own peculiar religion and in the end lived alone, deserted by his own fellows. Or else they died or were murdered. I don't know.' She shrugged. 'Just a story, maybe, and if you ask me, what the master believes is more likely; that in the old days it was quarried for slate by someone who didn't know what he was about. Because all good slate's in the north.'

'Oh.'

'Now don't go thinking things,' the old woman continued reprovingly. 'Wales is full of legends, and history – some true, some false. You've got to have imagination to appreciate the real Wales – but it's the true things that are richest in drama, and more fulfilling to know about. You go for those.' She paused for a moment while I wondered about her fund of language and clever way of putting facts.

'Did you know,' she continued, 'that Howell Harris himself lies not so very far away, buried in Talgarth's ancient churchyard. Fourteenth century *that* dates from, and Harris, in case you've never heard of him, was one of the great religious revivalists with John Wesley?'

'No,' I agreed, 'I didn't know.'

'Well, now you *do*. Yes, indeed. For that's facts, learned by me from my own grandmother.'

The longer I knew Mrs Maddox the more I realised what a fund of wisdom lay beneath her homely exterior. I think she must have sensed my changing inner attitude towards Owain.

Outwardly the brusqueness remained between us, but in spite of my determination not to be hurt by his curt tongue on occasion, obviously she knew I was.

'Take no notice,' she said one evening at the end of
October following an unfair comment on my appearance
when I'd returned from a walk with baskets of blackberries
for bottling. 'There's nothing wrong with your looks,
mistress – except to tease and worry him, looking as you
do with your cheeks rosy and black hair loose. When
jealousy hits a man he can say hard things and that's a fact.'

'*Jealous*? Of *me*?' I laughed shortly; the mockery of a
sound.

'That's what I said.'

I simply stared at her, then remarked half in curiosity,
half bitterness, 'Why should he be? And of whom? It isn't
as if – you know very well what our marriage is and how it
began. And Mistress Tripton! *She's* the one he wanted. *She*
knows it, *I* know it, *you* know it. Please, Mrs Maddox, don't
try and deny it now. I've had to accept the truth, and there
it is. So don't suggest Owain and I will ever be close. If I
could give him a son he'd be kinder no doubt. But that
doesn't seem to happen. Well –' I shrugged, ' – maybe
after Merionne it's for the best. To have a boy like her
would only make things worse.'

'Fiddlesticks! rubbish!' Mrs Maddox snapped. 'Fear like
that's *wrong*, girl. Think properly, or better still, don't
think at all, and you may get what you both want. Another
thing –' She lifted a finger, poking her head forward from
her old shoulders, 'When next he comes to the bedroom
be welcoming and soft. *Smile*. Be yourself and forget the
resentful proud Madam Geraint with a chip on her
shoulder.

Her optimistic sound good sense registered at last. I
forced all grudges to the back of my mind, and decided to
take her advice when the next opportunity arose.

I didn't have to wait long.

The following evening Owain came to me.

I was almost ready for bed, and had not expected him.
My chemise was already off, and I was sitting before the

dressing table mirror with my hair loose about my bare shoulders. My corsets had been thankfully removed and lay carelessly on the bed with the rest of my underwear. Hearing the creaking of the door, I grabbed a wrap quickly and was pulling it round me when Owain, carrying a candle, entered. The fitful flames lit his lean countenance eerily. He looked purposeful, yet younger than usual somehow, with a gleam lighting his dark eyes that told me what he had come for. My heart and body leaped. Embarrassed, which was ridiculous really, I rose from the stool.

'Stay there,' he said, putting the candle down and coming towards me, 'I'll carry you.'

The dressing wrap he wore parted as he strode towards me, revealing unashamedly the firm strong contours of his body. I could feel the warm blood coursing through my veins in a rising tide of crimson. Instinctively I took a step backwards and almost stumbled.

He laughed softly. 'Olwen, Olwen. Why so virginal? It isn't the first time.'

One hand of his was behind, at the base of my neck then caressing my skull where the thick hair fell; the other at my waist above the soft curve of buttocks, pulling me closer and closer, while a great thrill trembled through me. At the same moment the loose garment – my one defence – fell to the ground, leaving me naked as he. Naked and ready. Oh, yes, I was ready, with a tumultuous hunger that blinded and swept me to submission.

He lifted and carried me to the wide bed where I lay with his golden-brown body on mine, strong and demanding, seeking the deepest fountain of my being that pulsed to meet him. From the lush throbbing dark, our bodies and inmost spirits became one. He was ruthless, yet kind, with a wildness about him that was also caressingly soft, as soft as the deep blue velvet touch of a summer's night. And while we drowned and rose again in that pool of ecstasy, entwined and bound, lips on lips, flesh in flesh, sighs and words of endearment broke intermittently from him, Welsh words and avowals of love unknown to me, but holding all the wonder of the loveliest music ever heard.

And then, at last, when we lay at peace, it happened.

The terrible thing that was to bring such disaster to our new-found rapture.

I was lying sweetly exhausted in a stage of half-dream with one of Owain's legs loosely over my stomach, a hand playing gently with my hair, when I said it. That one awful word, spoken so innocently and meaning nothing, yet in impact causing a complete collapse of everything I'd dreamed of for so long. Satisfied, and at rest, my mind was playing this way and that, looking back chiefly, realising how futile and ineffectual life had been until this one heady hour. I had never before remotely imagined what true commitment between a man and woman could be. My earlier 'awakening' had been a child's dream, a fairytale, with nothing to it but sentiment and perhaps – blue butterflies.

I think I must have been smiling a little, when Owain's firm hand tightened on a breast and he said softly, 'Cariad – oh, cariad –'

'Cariad,' I echoed unthinkingly, 'that's what Bryn used to call me.'

Instantly there was a withdrawing of the hand, a jerking movement as Owain tore himself away, sat up, and said in tones I couldn't recognise. '*What* did you say? *Bryn*? Was that it? Bryn?'

I stared up at him in astonishment, 'I – I may have. Don't – don't *look* like that, Owain. Darling, it was nothing – *meant* nothing. I was just thinking how stupid –'

He didn't let me finish; there was a hard hateful bitter look on his face before he sprang out of bed and stood looking down on me in such anger I thought he'd strike me. But he didn't. He merely said, breathing hard, 'So that was it. While you lay there so wild and willing it wasn't with me, was it? All the time it was your old lover, the one who bedded you before me. You've never forgotten, have you? Damn your lovely eyes and lying red lips. Damn him and your sly smart cheating ways. Such a clever little madam you've been, haven't you these last years? Pretending innocence and respect for me, making me believe you were really wanting me at last, when all the time –' He broke off suddenly, turned away, reached for his wrap and slung it savagely round him.

I jumped from the bed and ran after him as he went to the door, crying, 'Owain, listen, listen – I can explain –' I grabbed his arm but he pushed me back and marched from the room with a slam of the door. I fell on the tumbled sheets feeling sobs of despair fill my throat. That such a *little* thing – just Bryn's name – could wreak such havoc! I couldn't believe it.

But I did.

I had to.

Because in the morning Owain had gone away.

He was absent for just one week, no one knew where. When he returned he gave no explanation. Neither did I or Mrs Maddox ask for one. The tight set of his features and remote cold manner forebade questioning of his affairs.

But I couldn't help wondering if Mistress Tripton was concerned.

VII

For a time, following the unpleasant bedroom scene Owain kept out of my sight as much as possible, spending further short periods away, presumably in Cardiff or Newport, and when he *did* return to Llangarrack it was with the fury of work once more upon him, and a rigid determination to see that everyone employed on the estate, including extra labourers for harvesting and field work during that busy season, put every minute and ounce of energy he had into the reaping. The estate was thriving. In the last two years several acres of common land on the southern side of the house sloping downwards towards the valley had been enclosed by Owain for agriculture. He had sent for a new steam traction engine to deal with future ploughing and farming operations, also a threshing machine, which must have cost a good deal.

I knew also from gossip overheard from the men, that a large stretch of rough heath had been enclosed as part of Llangarrack estate – which already comprised 2,000 acres – for setting alight, ready for cultivation in the spring. Crops and sheep were steadily increasing the Geraint income; but I knew that even if he did not need the extra revenue, Owain's obsession remained for reclaiming also the expanse of grazing pasture 'stolen' – he would have no other word for it than 'stolen' – by the Tripton family. He must have his herd, at whatever price, to better the English usurpers.

So there was no feeling of relaxation about the house. I

felt bitter. If only he could give me one friendly smile – make one gesture that he was willing to listen and be reasonable about my stupid slip of Bryn's name following our love-making! But he did not. Any sign or show of warmth from him, in rare moments of contact, was for Merionne. Obviously her beauty entranced him, together with her dumbness, acquiescience, and slow sweet smile that on occasion I found so irritating. There could be another reason for my sharp words, too, I told myself darkly. Maybe her silken fairness reminded him of Eleanor Tripton. At such moments I almost disliked my own child, wanted to cry, 'What's the matter with you? Why do you stare like that? Why can't you be normal, and shout, and laugh, scream sometimes, like other young things? And why must you follow Owain around? He's not your father. He's not, he's *not*. You're mine alone.'

But, of course, I didn't. I did the best I could to see she had all she wanted and was well dressed and cared for. She had one habit that worried me of wandering away when she had the chance, towards the tower which seemed to have an undue fascination for her. Once, having lost sight of her for a short time, I found her half way up the track there, standing as though in a dream, staring towards the high ridge of mountain bordering the two countries and the Tripton estate beyond. Almost simultaneously, against the glitter of hazed sunlight, I noticed something else; the poised dark figure of a woman on a black horse.

Eleanor.

The recognition between us, I'm sure, despite the distance, was mutual. For some seconds we all stood perfectly static, watching. Then, with a sudden quick movement the animal and its mount took a sharp turn and disappeared into the quivering haze of the horizon.

I took Merionne's hand, gripping it so hard she winced.

'Come along,' I said, 'you've no right here, do you understand?' Then, shamed by the wide-eyed innocence of her gaze, I added, 'Oh, Merionne, why can't you *speak*? Why can't we understand each other?'

She shook her head mutely. Compassion and guilt flooded me. Compassion for her inability to comprehend, guilt because I could so resent it, and perhaps because I so harshly grudged her affection for Owain.

After that I saw Eleanor on more than one occasion cantering across the heath, and suspicions began to niggle me that she was on the watch for my husband.

One afternoon I said tentatively to Mrs Maddox, 'Mrs Tripton seems to enjoy riding the heath around the tower. I suppose it's a habit of hers?'

The old lady gave me a sidelong shrewd glance.

'I don't keep a watch for the likes of that flighty madam,' she said cryptically. 'Seeing much of the mountain's common land she's as much right to use it as any other.' When I said nothing, she queried sharply, 'Why? What makes you ask?'

I shrugged.

'I just thought – well – oh, never mind. Nothing really.'

She snapped her teeth on a thread of cotton she was sewing with, and retorted quickly, 'You thought the master and she might be meeting out there? If you are, forget it. It's my belief he's not the use for her he once had. But if they get together for a chat occasionally there's nothing *you* can do about it but act more loving to him than you seem to be doing these days.'

I pulled myself together abruptly and retorted with an attempt at dignity, 'It's hardly your place to speak in that way, Mrs Maddox.'

'Speaking out of turn can do a deal of good sometimes,' she said, 'and I'm sure, mistress, young as you are, you're not above taking a bit of good advice.'

'No. That's true; I'm sorry. I didn't mean to sound haughty.'

'No need for apology. Remember one thing, though –

I've known the master a lifetime longer than you have. Nursed him when he was but a bit of a babe in the cradle, and a proud wilful one he was then; oh, yes, indeed. Thirty-seven years ago – but the stubbornness is still there, and you'll never break it by suspicions and telling him what to do and what not. Charm him you may, in time, if you think it's worth the trouble.' She paused, then added, watching my face carefully and added, 'It's my belief, as you well know, that you've done it already. What's gone wrong between you is *your* affair. But the sooner you right it, the quicker that wanton wild-cat of a woman will be off the scene.'

'Wildcat', I thought, what an odd way of describing the elegant, exquisite Mrs Tripton. And yet when I considered the remark further I realised there was a certain aptness in it. The sensual grace of movement, watchful enigmatic glance at the luminous slanting eyes and secretive little half-smile, held a strange feline quality that was both intimidating and calculated to bewitch for her own ends.

I would never trust her an inch. No, I certainly wouldn't, I determined. She had ensnared Owain once, and the enchantment had never entirely died – I was sure of it. But I would never, *never* let her get her claws on him again if I could help it. I would try harder to follow the advice of Mrs Maddox and soften the breach between us. He *had* loved me and shown it on that fatal night before my stupid gaffe concerning Bryn. *And I was his wife.* That very evening I'd forget all hurt pride, and somehow get him to the bedroom, tell him perhaps that I had some serious matter to discuss. I'd *beg* him to spare me a few minutes if I had to. But it was important to have a credible excuse. The difficulty was – *what?* There was one genuine question I could put to him: that of my parentage. My identity. I could say it had worried me always, and sometimes I grew moody because of it – suggest perhaps that I was troubled about whether or not my ancestry in any way could account for Merionne's oddness.

Yes. *Yes*. That was it. Beneath his hardness he was a reasonable man, up to a point. He might even tell me the truth in which case a double purpose would be served by such a meeting.

Now I really had a plan, something that must surely break the deadlock of our relationship, my spirits soared.

And although Owain looked doubtful, a little nonplussed when I cornered him in the hall later, and asked in what I hoped was a most reasonable and adult manner for a few words with him before retiring, a tiny frown creased his forehead as he said, 'I have a great deal of business to attend to this evening, Olwen. If you want to come into the library now –'

'Oh, no, no,' I said quickly. 'Later please. In the bedroom I thought. I wouldn't take long, you see –'

'The *bed*room? Now what's got into you? It seems a very strange and sudden request to make at this period of our warring existence.'

I tried not to blush.

'It isn't that.'

'What?'

'Not what you think.'

'My dear Olwen, you can have no possible idea of what I'm thinking – or maybe you have. If so, you've a nerve. Now let us adjourn this proposition till tomorrow, if you don't mind.'

'I do mind,' I said stubbornly, 'and I've only suggested the bedroom because no one would hear. It's – it's very private.'

'Oh, very well,' he said curtly. 'I'll come upstairs in my own time when I've dealt with a certain pressing matter. Or maybe before.'

'No. Not earlier,' I told him. 'I won't – you see I've things to do too. Putting Merionne to bed and seeing she's asleep. If you could make it about ten, Owain?'

He sighed, and I knew he was irritated by what must have appeared my childishness. I'd probably put things wrongly and sounded ridiculously naive. He might even have seen through me, but I didn't think so. How could he? When what I was about to do was so uncharacteristic of the Olwen March he'd married.

Seduction.

That was the word.

I was planning to seduce my own husband.

*

Hearing the firm heavy tread of his footsteps along the passage I rushed to the mirror for a last glance of my carefully prepared reflection. Oh, so different from the unsophisticated image I was used to seeing. My flannelette nightdress was unbuttoned at the neck showing a glimpse of white skin below the slight hollow at the base of my throat. Through the soft flickering candlelight my red lips were slightly parted where two small teeth gleamed with a pearly sheen. I'd darkened my brows and lashes with make-up, and tipped my high cheekbones with rouge, cosmetics that I'd bought secretly at a perfumery in Newport during the one occasion Owain had taken me there on one of his business trips. Since then they'd been kept safely away from prying eyes in a little box for trinkets which had a key. It had been a present from Widow Price on my fifteenth birthday, intended, she said, for any small gifts or treasures my future husband might give me. An optimistic remark.

I'd had nothing from him but handkerchiefs on occasion, a comb to keep my hair in order, and a small book in which my daily duties were to be clearly marked, and a face cloth. No perfume or 'pretty fallals', as he called them, just dull but useful articles.

So while he was involved in a discussion with a business acquaintance in the bar parlour of an inn, I'd been given permission to visit the Apothecary's over the road to get some special ointment that Mrs Maddox wanted. And it was then that I'd also slipped in the perfumery.

How gratified I felt now, that the minor extravagances were proving of some use, and that Owain, that week being in a good mood, had not thought it necessary to have an accurate and detailed account of how my household allowance had been spent.

Until the drastic decision to use such artifices had been made, I'd almost forgotten the existence of the small packets and tiny pots of paint. Now their full importance registered. I was transformed. A different person. My eyes, rimmed with kohl, looked enormous. I'd applied the shadow carefully, and powdered my face so the highly-placed rouge blended into the natural cream of my skin. My dark hair was pinned on top of my head intertwined with scarlet ribbon, as scarlet as my lips. I had no earrings, of course, the Widow Price would have considered such adornment wicked folly in the 'sight of the Lord'. And there'd been no money or opportunity for purchasing any in Newport. In any case, my ears weren't pierced. Round my neck I placed a thin gold chain with a cross hanging from it – the one expensive present ever given to me by my foster-mother. Through the candlelight it glinted as a symbol of purity. But somehow I didn't *look* pure at all. The small glistening object lying just above the soft curves of my breast, suggested a certain youthful voluptuousness that pleased me. Would it please Owain? I bit my underlip staring apprehensively yet with excitement, as I considered his reaction to the new Olwen Geraint. It would be a surprise to him, of course. Perhaps a shock, when I went towards him, letting the loose wrap fall away from bare shoulders over only a low-cut camisole, and frilly petticoat – my very best.

'Oh, Owain,' I thought half-turning and looking towards the door. 'You must *like* me. You *must*.' And I imagined his look of astonishment giving place to admiration – the sudden realisation that his young wife had become a woman grown, in her own way equally, if not more attractive, than the haughty, detestable Eleanor Tripton.

In the last second of waiting, my heart quickened uncontrollably so I could hardly breathe.

The door opened. He came in, slamming the door behind him.

I smiled, letting the hand at my neck fall away. He simply stood staring for a moment while I took several steps in his direction and held out my arms.

I think I said, 'Owain.' Just one word, but he made no response at first. I swallowed nervously, sensing something was not quite right. It was as though he was struck dumb. Then I babbled on heedlessly, 'I wanted to ask you something – something very important to me – something you must know and I don't – about – about myself. Who *am* I? My parents? Oh, *please* –' I hardly knew what I was talking about any more. His reaction was so completely different from what I'd hoped and made myself expect.

His complete silence terrified me. 'What's the matter?' I cried. 'Don't look like that.'

Then he moved, and went to the ewer, took a cloth, plunged it in, and strode to my side, grabbed me by one shoulder, and with his other hand first slapped my face, not hard, but sharply, before scrubbing my cheeks with the icy towel.

I tried to escape but he held me cruelly until all traces of my so carefully applied make-up must have been rubbed away. Following the undignified procedure he pushed me on to the stool before the mirror, and standing behind me said, 'There! take a good look at yourself. That's what you are – a slut. Just as your mother was before you. She was a trollop. Understand? A no-good street-walker. And your father was a drunken fop, the son of a wealthy squire who sent him abroad to save the honour of the family. They're both dead now. Your grandfather, too, who showed considerable generosity in ensuring you were provided for. Not many would have done it. Certainly not me in his place. So now you know. And maybe knowing it, you'll rid yourself for good of any high-flown ideas of noble ancestry, and make a show of decent behaviour. You'd better, by God. Because I don't intend to maintain a trumpery, audacious little wanton at Llangarrack.'

His face, thrust forward over my head stared cold and hard at me from the mirror. I looked a sight, with wisps of wet hair hanging limply over my smudged countenance. Water, which could have been partly tears tricked in dark streaks over the cheekbones where rouge had been so carefully applied. My lips trembled painfully from the scrubbing they'd received.

'And don't ever let me see you like that again,' he resumed more quietly, releasing me. 'You may have ensnared your precious Bryn in such a way, but if you ever try it again on me you'll get such a walloping you'll never forget. Now get up. Cover yourself and don't dare come downstairs again until you're modestly and decently clad. Understand?'

I nodded dumbly.

'Very well.' That one short sentence of his ended the dreadful encounter.

He turned to leave, and on the way out of the room pulled aside the brief curtain which shielded Merionne's cot from the rest of the room. She was sleeping peacefully as she always did, looking like an angelic cherub, completely unconcerned by affairs outside her dreamlike world of limited understanding.

For a second I hated them both for the chains imposed on me. But moments later I flung myself on the bed, gripping the sheets between clenched hands, sobbing painfully.

Nothing had gone right for me, everything was desperately wrong. Too wrong now ever to be put right again, I thought hopelessly. But I would survive, yes I would, even if it was just to pay Owain out one day for the terrible things he'd said and done.

Following the unpleasant incident I avoided Owain's presence as much as possible, as he likewise avoided mine. He seldom came to my room. Intimacy between us was rare, a bitter experience without love merely endured for one purpose, his obsession for begetting a son.

I realised, grudgingly, how foolish my naive attempt at allure had been; I should have recalled the former scene when the very name of Bryn had caused such anger. But he had been cruel and ruthless in a way no man should be to his wife. And his reference to my mother! I didn't believe him. I just *didn't*. He should apologise, I told myself time after time. What about Eleanor Tripton anyway? Who was Owain to sit in judgement?

As the days went by I became convinced, rightly or wrongly, that they met secretly at the dark tower up the lane which had become a symbol to me of forbidden trysts and lurking danger. Very occasionally, unbeknown to Owain, I took a quick walk that way and once saw old Huw, the shepherd, pushing through the tangled entrance with a bundle under his arm. He gave a brief nod when he saw me, and a gesture of greeting with his hand. It wasn't often he was seen in the valley – the flock was halfway up a slope beyond the treacherous shining pool where it was said a demon waited. Perhaps he bedded down on rare occasions in the tower, I thought idly, when winter mists or snow were thick about the mountains. But the suggestion somehow didn't tally with the subtle suggestion of feminine perfume and presence haunting the place.

Or, for that matter, with Owain's peculiar possessive attitude which had suggested I kept away from the vicinity. There was much that puzzled and depressed me at that time. Master Tripton and Eleanor made an unexpected visit to Llangarrack one afternoon, at which I naturally had to appear for tea, after hurriedly changing from my calico day dress into a modest high-necked gown of fine woollen material. My hair was taken severely from my face, and no ornament was worn for adornment. Beside Eleanor in a wine-coloured riding habit, I felt dull, a drab, and caught Owain's eye on me speculatively with a hint of gratification in it, thinking, no doubt, he'd succeeded in taming me.

Well, in a way so he had; not really by his threats of a beating, but through the cold sterile days of his rejection.

I behaved decorously, I think, over refreshments, and with chill politeness, which brought an ironic gleam to Mistress Tripton's lovely eyes.

Afterwards Owain said to me, 'Congratulations.'

'On what?'

'Behaving for once as you should.'

A sudden rush of anger seized me. I was tempted to a show of temper, but managed to control any words or actions which would only have resulted in a further scene. *Why – why* couldn't he have made one remark to me without a barb in it? There had been a chance. A simple opportunity to restore – or rather build – a friendly relationship. But no.

He was hateful. Cold, cruel, and indifferent where I was concerned. So I would be the same.

After that matters worsened. There was little conversation between us except when a remark was needed in front of the staff to dispel gossip. But that was seldom necessary. Owain and I lived as hostile occupants under one roof, and I was very careful to show by my contemptuous expression whenever we passed in the hall, stairs, or landing, that his presence was distasteful to me. I didn't want him near.

He knew it, and behaved likewise.

All the same, when there was time, and he was about Llangarrack acres, goading the men to harder work and putting every ounce of energy into tilling, sowing, hedging, and all the endless preparation of land for new crops, I kept as careful a watch as possible on his comings and goings about the estate, with my eyes intermittently on the far ridge half expecting to see the silhouetted figure of a woman on a black horse cantering along the moor. A stubborn, almost ruthless desire to know the truth – have farther evidence of his duplicity haunted most of my waking thoughts. Though I dreaded the answer, should his continued falseness and obsession with the feline Tripton woman be proved true, then I'd have a certain power over him, and I'd use it in any way possible as revenge for his calling me 'a *slut*' and his hard treatment during the years of our marriage. Not a pleasant manner of thought, but I was no longer a pleasant person, and realised it. Perhaps later – oh, probably given the chance, the hardness in me could be melted and there would still be time for Owain and me to find some sort of mutual harmony.

Meanwhile I watched.

The weeks passed. Christmas came and went, under a false show of festivity; a brief period in which for the sake of the staff and Merionne a spread of more sumptuous food was prepared, more candles and lamps shone, and presents delivered from a tree.

I was thankful when it was over.

At the end of January the portion of healthland was set alight as planned, for future cultivation, and continued burning for two days and nights. There was something pagan and wildly beautiful about the red blaze lighting the eastern sky that brought sightseers from all around the district to watch from a safe angle. My spirits, stirred by the dramatic scene, lifted a little.

But on the Thursday following I had a shock. Something, at the moment, I was quite unprepared for. Owain was in Newport for the day, and taking the opportunity of not being stopped, I put on my thick cape for a sharp walk up the valley, leaving Merionne in Mrs Maddox's care.

The weather had turned cold during the day, silvering the landscape with frosted mist. An exhilarating tangy scent filled the air of crisp earth and decayed rot of leaves covering the ground where new shoots and life were already pushing towards the light. The fading sky held a greenish glow above the silhouetted rising humps of mountains. A strange sort of excitement filled me, and at moments I quickened my footsteps, sniffing the cold bitter-sweetness deep through my nostrils into my lungs.

I walked further than I'd meant to, and when I returned it was almost dark. Single lights, like fallen stars, twinkled from the valley below, and when I neared Llangarrack I noticed a yellowish glow from a side window, one that would not be seen from the lane, but could be visible only from an abrupt curve in the track, and from my position at a greater height.

The small parlour, I thought at first. One seldom used, but probably Mrs Maddox was fiddling round, tidying up, or looking for thread which was kept in the drawer of a small chest there. I shrugged and ambled on a few yards more slowly.

And then it happened.

There was movement behind the window. The mellow glow dimmed for a second, then lifted as blurred figures came into view – not clearly, merely shadowed shapes – two of them – a man's, which I knew by familiarity and instinct was Owain, then a woman's.

My heart lurched, stopped a beat, and then went on again, racing in a wild tattoo against my ribs.

Eleanor Tripton.

Though indistinct, filmed by a gauze of lace curtain, the arch of her neck and head surmounted by plumes, was unmistakable. Only shadows, both of them; but real, so *real*.

Slowly then, like a nightmare figure in a dream or play, she lifted her arm and glided towards him. He stood as though spellbound, while the two shadows became one – a single blurred shape, quite motionless, until a flicker of a lamp or candlelight gave movement, and a hand pulled a dark blind over the scene.

Then I knew.

And the knowledge was sickening. Far more chilling and terribly final than I'd ever envisaged. I felt almost faint. For a minute, perhaps less, I stood with eyes closed, leaning against a tree; then I forced myself to move, and feeling nothing but an empty sense of desolation and loss, made my way back to Llangarrack.

Owain was assisting Mistress Tripton to mount her horse when I arrived. Both glanced at me, making perfunctory remarks which meant nothing. A minute later she had gone – an elegant dark shape cantering down the lane on her splendid black mare.

I was too proud to accuse or question. There would have been no point anyway, since I already had the answer.

My husband also remained silent about the meeting.

Silence had become a sword between us.

VIII

At three years old, Merionne, though docile as ever, became more and more of a responsibility. On every opportunity she slipped away on some secret little wander of her own, though Mrs Maddox and I did our best to keep an eye on her. But she was quick on her feet, and though speechless still, her brain was nimble in escape and evasion whenever opportunity arose. It was impossible to keep an eye on her every moment of the day, as I pointed out to Owain when she was discovered by the old shepherd gathering wild flowers on one occasion in the vicinity of the tower.

'Acting a bit strange she was,' he told the housekeeper, when he brought her back holding her small hand in his. 'Making signs as though someone was with her. Odd little thing, oh, yes indeed.' He shook his head woefully.

Owain got to hear of the incident of course. 'Surely you have time to keep an eye on the child,' he said to me sharply. 'You don't have much else to do these days. Not even in the dairy.'

'I have sewing, a certain amount of cooking, and management of domestic affairs,' I replied with a hint of temper. 'The trouble is it's impossible to have any discipline or conversation with her. She's like some little wild animal always on the alert to slip away and hide.'

'Perhaps because she senses you've no real interest or heart for her,' he suggested drily.

'No heart for my own *child*?'

'Well, *have* you?'

He looked at me very directly.

I bit my lip and was silent for a moment, then I answered, 'If I hadn't I wouldn't bother as I do. I *did* love her, oh yes, and you know I did, at first. But trying and coping with a child that gives no response and can't communicate is wearying.'

'Much in life is,' came the answer, 'but nothing's achieved without effort.'

Impatience overcame me. 'Oh, don't sound so *stuffy* and preachified.'

I wanted to add, 'What about *you*? Has it every occurred to you that an effort could be made on *your* part to overcome your obsession for Eleanor Tripton?' But I was wise enough to refrain.

Owain's eyes already had a hot glow of temper in them as he replied, 'Watch your tongue. You're becoming a bit of a shrew these days, and that I'll not have in my own house. You understand?'

I said nothing. He sighed, and added, 'Your continued coolness and bitter temper doesn't improve your appearance. Take a good look at yourself in the mirror. You're growing hard-faced, Olwen. If there was warmth between us –' He broke off and shrugged, and in the short pause I said, unthinkingly:

'No one can pretend warmth where it isn't there. The lack is mutual, I think. I know you grudge me the fact that I haven't given you a precious son. Why don't you try elsewhere?'

His lips tightened.

'If it wasn't that staff were about the house I'd give you the sound beating you've been asking for, this long time. As it is, for my own dignity, if not yours, I'll refrain this time and go and think over what you've said. Yes, that's the answer; maybe you're right, madam. We shall have to see, won't we?'

And he walked away leaving me resentful, bitter, and chiding myself for being a fool.

*

Surprisingly, one day in full summer when all was gold about the landscape around the deep lilac shadowed bowls of mountains, Owain offered to take me on a trip to the vicinity of Nanty-Clyd. 'I've mining business in the next valley,' he said, 'and if you want a jaunt out we can have a lift with Farmer Thomas to Merthyr and get the steam train from there. The same on return.'

I stared at him.

'Oh, yes, of *course*,' I exclaimed immediately. 'I've often wondered what it looked like now. And there may be *someone* I remember.'

'We shan't have time for you to go visiting,' he told me, 'even if there was anyone left there you knew. Maybe it's a mistake on my part to let you go harping on old times, but perhaps a glimpse of the place as it is now will help clear your mind of the past.'

Knowing his last words referred to Bryn, I retorted sharply, 'I stopped remembering a long time ago. When I left, it was to make a new life, and so it's been.'

'Not altogether to your liking though,' he remarked in a voice strangely quiet for him, 'or to me. However –' He broke off, continuing after a moment, 'There's no point in regrets or conjecture. It's settled then. We're meeting Thomas at the village. So see you're dressed fit for a bit of walking. No fancy boots to slither about the stones, and have a suitable cape and bonnet to cover yourself. It's fine now, but my senses tell me there may be rain later.'

And so it was.

William Thomas was a well-to-do farmer living some miles away from Llangarrack, and his waggon was handsomely equipped to take a passenger or two as well as produce if necessary. I gathered that there would be no charge for our trip which was one of the reasons, probably, I told myself wrily, that Owain had accepted the offer instead of wasting Llangarrack horse energy for the Geraint landau. The family vehicle needed painting and repairing anyway, and would take a man from the fields and his job. In such minor matters Owain still seemed to me very mean.

It was afternoon when following the jaunt with the farmer we boarded the puffing steam train which took us in a circular direction towards Nanty-Clyd, stopping at halts en route, where small hamlets crouched against the sides of the rising hills, scarred by workings iron-grey under the sky. At last the squat small 'station' I'd known in my youth came into view, shadowed by the looming shape of the mountain beyond. There was the grinding of brakes as the train drew in; Owain opened the carriage door, stepped out to the platform, and offered a hand to help me down. I took it, there was a whistle, and a jolting grating of wheels as the train jerked to life again with a puffing of coiled steam thickening the air. The halt, some distance from Nanty-Clyd itself, had a desolate air.

I rubbed my eyes and adjusted my bonnet which had loosened from the jump down the deep step, and then my body stiffened in bewilderment.

I stared, hardly believing what I saw. On the opposite side of the valley mines still worked; there were rows of cottages flanking the curve of hill, forming the hamlet of Penytal. At the far bend of the circular railtrack were the remains of Nanty-Clyd on the right, which I recognised. But instead of the certain district I remembered, was a sheet of water, clear as dark glass, reflecting light and shade of the sky above, and of other things – other things surely, than clouds passing fleetingly across the fitful sun. For there I had walked and played with Marged and Bryn, gone to school and attended Sunday services at the small Methodist Chapel with the Widow Price. Somewhere beneath that wide expanse of water must be Polly the Post's shop, or what remained of it. Polly – did she lie there too, I wondered? Or had her kindly body been rescued and given a decent Christian burial? Involuntarily, as I stood there, speechless, my hand reached out, to be enclosed by Owain's firmly.

'Changed, isn't it?' I heard him say. 'The families that survived have new houses now, nearer Penytal. The lake's going to be purified properly and used for a reservoir. That's what I heard.'

I released my hand.

'But the mountain,' I said at last, 'where the Rhys-Evanses lived – it's – it's so different.' And I recalled with nostalgic pain the winding path above the farm leading through heather to the top; the picnics, and games, wild pansies and blue butterflies – school outings and the children I'd known. And Bryn. Bryn, of course. Marged, too, who'd been so scared of the family gander. Once it had torn her pinafore and still rushed squawking after her with a great frill round its neck like a ruffle.

Now the farm had gone. That side of the slope was sheer; majestic in a kind of wild way, but somehow frightening.

'I wonder if *any* of them are left?' I heard myself saying mechanically.

'No. I told you, I checked. I got a list of survivors. The Rhys-Evans, the postmistress, and the whole school were wiped out, with the Widow Price and her neighbours. Only a small portion of folk on the far side escaped, and I doubt you'd know them or they'd remember you. Well!' He gave me a look and added, 'You thought me hard when I stopped you making a visit at the time. I had reasons, hadn't I? You were resentful and gloomy enough without extra brooding over such tragedy.' He paused. 'There's a memorial cemetery near Penytal with names of those who lost their lives, including your Bryn.'

Controlling my voice with difficulty, I said coldly, 'Please don't.'

I could feel his eyes on me, and heard him saying in cool remote tones, 'So you still feel for him. I thought so.'

'I feel for them all. And I don't – I don't *really* know why you've brought me here after all this time.'

'Maybe a test,' he said more lightly. 'Cruel, perhaps. But you certainly jumped at the suggestion.'

I swallowed hard and forced my gaze from the mountain to the winding railway track leading round a diverted course, over a newly built bridge. And it seemed as I stared that the faint echo of singing – singing – was born on a chill rising wind ruffling the water.

'When is the train returning?' I asked, to break the sadness.

He reached for his fob and glanced at the gold watch hanging there.

'A quarter of an hour. What would you like to do in the meantime? Take a stroll down the back lane. The undergrowth has renewed itself, and I'm told the scenery is quite spectacular now.'

How *could* he? I thought. How could he lack the sensitivity to realise even a *little* of the nostalgia filling me. *Spectacular!* – such a terrible way of describing a scene risen from death and sorrow.

I shook my head.

'I'll stay here. I've seen enough.'

'Good.'

We perched ourselves on the seat outside the shelter and waited until the small branch train returned. 'There'll be another change at the main station,' Owain remarked. 'But the rest of the journey's short, and my business won't take long – quarter of an hour at the most.'

'I see.'

'What's the matter? Tired?'

I shook my head.

'Just thinking.'

'Ah.' He turned away in mild irritation, his profile sternly set under its stove hat.

'You *would* come,' he reminded me once again. 'I think I warned you it wouldn't exactly be a pleasant jaunt.'

'Yes, you did. I don't regret it. It's just that everything seems so – *strange*.'

And indeed it did.

In a kind of dream I recall boarding the little train again when it returned, of arriving at the larger station, and from there riding in a cab down cobbled streets to a row of commercial buildings overlooking a canal. The horses pulled up before the taller of these. Owain told me to wait in the vehicle until he came back. I saw him give orders to the jarvy, and a moment later his tall figure was walking briskly up the steps and through the door, past a square window where the words 'J.E. Edwards and Co, Shipping', were emblazoned in gold lettering.

Another of Owain's financial interests, I thought vaguely, and wondered if he had ever been so limited in pocket as he'd stressed to everyone at Llangarrack.

Oddly, I wasn't really interested. I felt in a limbo, lost between two worlds. Sad and uncertain of my own identity – of where I really belonged.

It was as though my recent restless years as Owain Geraint's wife had absorbed the past into a mirage where only ghost shapes registered, shapes of pain resurrected fleetingly in imagination through the quivering waters of the lake.

The truth was, of course, that I was exhausted, and not only by the traumatic visit to Nanty-Clyd, but by the fact – although I did not know it then – that I was at last with child. A month passed before I was certain, and then I did not immediately tell Owain, as most women in my kind of circumstances would probably have done, but kept the knowledge to myself, my own secret until the right time came to divulge it.

It was during this period that Merionne's behaviour became more wilful and elusive. At one moment she seemed to understand what I was saying, the next a faraway look would be in her eyes, and unless watched carefully she would have disappeared leaving the whole household edgy and searching for her. She was four years old, lovely as a child in a fairytale, and Owain adored her. The adoration was mutual, and there were many occasions during those first days of my pregnancy when I was tempted to break the annoying relationship between them by blurting out the truth. But I didn't. I was too proud to admit jealousy, although in my heart I knew it was there, and couldn't bear the idea of using my new power merely as a weapon. Whether she might have responded to firmer discipline, I never knew. The trouble was that Owain would allow none.

'She does no harm,' he said once to me sharply. 'She doesn't cry or make a noise or openly defy you. If you could show more true affection for her she'd stay close. Remember this, Olwen, I hold you responsible for her well-being and whereabouts. You haven't to be on her track *all* the time. She sleeps often in the afternoons, doesn't she? And when she *does* skip away occasionally it's only to somewhere like –'

'The tower?' I interrupted shortly, a little shrilly. 'Oh, yes. *Your* tower.'

Now why had I said that?

His face darkened.

He gave a short contemptuous cough, and turned away.

'I really don't know what's the matter with you. Sometimes I think you must be sick. No wonder the child clings to me.'

He strode out of the room. I heard a door slam, and only seconds later saw from the window his bold figure striding down the drive towards the fields.

The next day when I was in the dairy Merionne took the chance of making one of her swift escapes.

Exasperated, I went in search of her, and as I'd guessed she was roaming about the tower, and not alone. By her side was a grey hungry-looking dog, of no particular breed, but obviously intent on nuzzling and making friends with my daughter.

'Merionne –' I called sharply. 'You shouldn't have – come along, quickly. And leave that animal alone –'

She heard, and looked up at the sound of my voice, then approached tentatively, the dog by her side, its head slightly lowered either in fear or resentment. I went quickly forward and grasped her hand. So small it felt, and fragile under mine, cool and delicate as frail china. For a second she resisted, and I made a gesture of dismissal at the dog. It stared at me from golden eyes holding a curious look of appeal. Lost, I thought; a vagabond dog in search of food and a home. But it wouldn't be wanted at Llangarrack, and could be a danger to the sheep.

'Shoo!' I said. 'Go away – *away.*'

After a short pause in which Merionne broke free and touched its neck gently, the animal turned back up the lane, and fled with the speed of a fox, past the tower until its grey shape finally disappeared into the shadows of the mountains.

Merionne walked grudgingly back with me to Llangarrack.

Mrs Maddox was in the kitchen.

'Ah! so you've found her,' she exclaimed from her chair. 'Up the valley, I suppose.'

'Yes. And she had company. A dog looking like a half-wild creature. If you see it about, Mrs Maddox, send it away. My husband certainly wouldn't want it about the house, or old Huw, either.'

The old woman flung me an odd look. 'I don't reckon either of them would mind,' she said. 'If it's the same one as I think. Indeed no.'

'What do you mean?'

'It makes its way here when the mood takes it,' she said. 'The master bears it no grudge, nor Huw neither. The creature does no harm, and if you ask me, mistress, no evil will come of its affection for little Merionne. Eh, bach?' She smiled at the little girl in the confiding, knowing way ancient folk sometimes have for the very young.

'Do you mean my husband's seen it and allows it prowling about?'

'Let us say he's met it on more than one occasion and shown no objection.'

I shook my head.

'I just don't understand. If the dog's a stray it could easily go for the sheep, and what about our yard dog and Huw's collie?'

'They don't meet. That grey animal has sense.' She paused before adding, 'Mountain knowledge.'

I sighed. 'I just don't understand. No doubt you've fed and encouraged it, which is the chief reason it's lurking about Llangarrack. Well, I shall tell my husband what I think, and that I don't want it in contact with Merionne.'

'I wouldn't, mistress,' the housekeeper told me, a note of warning in her voice. 'Let friendship be, where friendship is. There's enough of bickering and resentment about as it is.'

'That's not my fault.'

'There you go again. Always arguing.'

Resentment churned in me.

'But you're blaming *me*. Why? – *Why?* Things haven't been easy, and you know it. I have *tried*.'

'There now,' her mood changed, became gentler, more conciliatory. 'I know, I know. Come. Sit yourself down and I'll get us a cup of something. For the child, too.' She glanced at Merionne who was standing by the table watching us solemnly as though taking in all that was said.

Her head drooped slightly; the limpid azure eyes turned upon us as though in reproach.

I shook my head. 'I think I should get her tidied up first, Mrs Maddox. Look at her dress, all messed with twigs and soil. If Owain saw her with her hair tangled and dirty hands he'd be annoyed. So –'

I didn't finish what I'd started to say because Owain came in, went straight across to Merionne and lifted her up in his arms, holding her so his eyes could stare straight into hers.

'And how's my lovely?' he asked. 'A little wild one today, is she? All sweet with grass and leaves?' He was smiling; all of a sudden the years had dropped from him leaving a younger, more vulnerable Owain than I had ever known.

He put her down and gave me a swift piercing glance. 'No trouble, I hope?' His tone was curt and chilling. It was as though the brief softening in him had turned to ice.

'As usual,' I retorted. 'Except that Merionne's found a new friend. A dog, which apparently you knew about.'

'Oh, that grey animal. Yes, I've seen it about occasionally. The roving kind. That's what I call him, Rover.'

'So he's even got a name.'

'Not officially. He's nameless, that one – no home, no mate that I know of. Born wild and free. One day in one place, the next another. Some folk in the district take him as a sign.'

'A *sign*? Of what?'

'Good luck.'

'But surely *you* don't hold such ridiculous superstitions?'

Owain shrugged. 'I never give it a thought. To me he's a part of the mountains, and I wouldn't want him harmed.'

'I hope you don't think *I'd* wish to harm any animal or human being,' I retorted. 'It's just that –' I broke off, suddenly recalling the feline sly glance of Eleanor Tripton's lovely cat-eyes. Would I harm *her*? Perhaps; a quick slap, no more.

'Yes? Just that – what?' I heard Owain question brusquely.

'Oh, nothing. Nothing at all. All right, if *you* don't mind the dog trailing round after Merionne I suppose we must put up with it.'

The discussion broke off there, and I pushed the matter from my mind as a mere unimportant incident having no real bearing at all on life at Llangarrack.

But I was wrong; dreadfully wrong, as the future was to prove.

IX

During the first early months of my pregnancy I felt fit physically except for occasional attacks of slight nausea which no one knew about. But one morning, having slept badly during the night, I had to leave the breakfast table and go to the kitchen door for a breath of air. The weather was dull and oppressive, with a leaden belt of cloud filming any sun there was. A curious sense of lassitude filled me. For a few moments the earth seemed to recede beneath my feet. I swayed and thought I would faint; but managed to recover by leaning against the sturdy wood, one hand gripping the knob.

The unpleasant moment was brief, though long enough to have raised speculation in Mrs Maddox's shrewd mind. Or perhaps she'd sensed the truth earlier and kept silent about it, I don't know. But when I returned she remarked with a knowing glint in her old eyes, 'You've hardly tasted your gruel, mistress. Come, now, sit down and take nourishment.' She paused before adding, 'It's my belief you need it. Peeky you look. Indeed so.' I seated myself mechanically while she glanced at Dilly who was at the far side near the large square of a window. 'Dilly, hurry up now with those few pots and get to the dairy. That floor needs a good scrubbing.'

When the girl had gone, and I'd pushed my bowl aside with only a little of the gruel tasted, she said conspiratorially, 'Is there something I should know, mistress? And the master, too, perhaps?'

'No, nothing,' I answered too decisively. 'Certainly not my husband. *Or* you, yet. At least –'

'Yes? Come now. It's many years I've lived, and during that time I've learned well to know the signs. You're with child, aren't you?'

I could feel the hot blood mounting my face in a deepening tide of crimson.

'And if I am?'

'Well, now, that's good news, isn't it?'

'I don't really know. It depends.'

'Now what do you mean by that?'

'If he – or she – turned out like Merionne it would be awful. And it so easily *could*.'

'Now that's a wicked way of looking at things, if I may say so. It's a fine healthy boy you'll have. These old bones of mine tell me so, providing, of course, you take care of yourself, eat well and wisely and do nothing foolish. But you should inform the master as soon as possible –'

'*No*.' My voice was emphatic. 'Not yet. And see *you* don't. That's an order.'

'But why, *why*, girl, when it's what he's been waiting for for so long?'

'I have my reasons,' I told her coldly, which was true, although by then they were becoming confused in my own mind. To deny him the gratification as long as I could? Was that the chief reason? Or the very real fear that some inherent weakness or taint in my mother's blood might have resulted in Merionne's pathetic shortcomings?

Recently I'd brooded overmuch on the latter problem. A slut, and worse – a street-walker he'd called her in his wild rage of the past when I'd made such a painted show of myself in order to impress and enchant him. Many times I'd been on the point of demanding an explanation, or some proof of the cruel words, but had always refrained, dreading his answer. Then, later the fear had lifted when reason told me that had my mother been in any way a sick woman Owain Geraint who wished healthy heirs for his name and estate would certainly not have married me. So he had been merely cruel and wishing to hurt me. Well, then, I would keep what was mine to myself till the truth had to come out.

But I knew now from the very slight thickening of my body it could not be for very long. And when the day came I would somehow pin him down and get an accurate account of my ancestry.

The weather continued grey and sultry; and at times little Merionne appeared to wilt. There was a sad quality about her then that aroused a feeling of guilt in me, guilt that the passionate love I'd felt for her during the first months of her fragile life could have changed almost unnoticed to resentment and impatience. The bond between us had become little more than duty on my part. Her beauty itself was an irritation, a symbol of my rejection by Bryn, and constant reminder of the woman who had become such a torment in my life, Eleanor Tripton.

Every time Owain touched the child's cheek with a finger or gave her an affectionate hug, I imagined him caressing the cat-like creature of his obsession. Afterwards I was ashamed of myself for such thoughts which could be excused only perhaps by the fact of my pregnancy, and that I secretly longed so deeply for Owain to love me.

It was the same with the dog. I only had very rare glimpses of it, and when I saw it, it shied away into the shadows of the mountains, its shape becoming lost in the distant grey of hills and sky. Yet with Owain it displayed a friendly relationship shutting me out.

Perhaps I was imagining things. Certainly at that time the atmosphere of place became intensified in my mind.

Mrs Maddox did her best to get me occupied in domestic practical tasks, although she still insisted that Owain should know of my condition.

'When he does,' I told her, following one of our arguments over the matter, 'I'll have no freedom at all. He'll want me cosseted and shut up in the house, having to rest and be watched over, just in case anything harms his precious son before it's born.'

'Now, now!' the old woman chided, 'it's wrong you are to go talking like that. The master isn't one for mollycoddling, as you well know, and from the look of you you need a bit of comfort and warmth. There should be peace between you at such a time.'

'*Peace?*' I gave a short, derisive mockery of a laugh. 'Can you imagine it, with *us*?'

'If you give him a chance I can,' she answered stubbornly. 'Sometimes I can't make you out at all; indeed no. When you first came here as his wife you seemed such an agreeable, willing young thing. Oh, there were moments of rebellion, yes. You had a brave spirit, and needed it. Nothing wrong in that. But gradually it's as though bitterness has got a hold on you eating your heart away, and taking the joy and beauty of you with it –' she broke off, shaking her head, then added, 'It's not right.'

'There's a reason though,' I remarked darkly. 'Merionne, being as she is – and that – that woman – Tripton's wife. It's no use saying all's over between them; it isn't. They meet up there by the tower and other places. I know it.'

'How? Have you seen them?'

'Yes. Here.'

'Here? Now, mistress you just tell me what you mean by that. I find it hard to believe things have been going on under my very nose that I'd no knowledge of.'

I described the incident of the shadowed embrace behind the window that I'd seen by a freak chance on my return from a walk.

'Owain must have returned earlier from Newport than expected,' I concluded. 'Where you were I don't know. But it happened.'

'And you said nothing to him?'

I shook my head.

'What use?'

She clucked between her teeth, then almost spitting with indignation said shrilly, 'Use? *Use?* If what you say is true and you weren't all bemused, you should've confronted him and had a good old set-to. I'm not one for bickering and quarrelling as you should know by now. But there's a time for everything. Clearing the air could've brought you together, and before you knew it you would've landed up in his arms. That's human nature. Like the fields and valleys – all fresh and tender, springing to new life after a good old storm. Well –' She paused, took a deep breath and continued, 'That's it then. If Master Owain's acting like a foolish boy sacrificing what's rich and waiting for him beneath his nose for a bundle of trash, then something should be done. And I'm going to do it.'

'What do you mean?'

'Either you tell that husband of yours his child's thriving in your belly – forgive my putting it like that – or I *will*. This very night.'

'You won't. You mustn't. I forbid it.' My heart was hammering angrily, although secretly something in me welcomed the opportunity for having things taken out of my hands.

'It's no good arguing, mistress. My duty's clear. When my mind's made up, I act.'

And so it was.

When I retired that evening, before going to bed, there was a knock on the bedroom door, and Owain entered.

I was standing at the window staring at the misted summer sky fading with a golden glow behind the mountains, only the bodice of my gown unloosed, my dark hair tumbled about my shoulders. I didn't move when he entered, or when he said, 'Olwen? What's this I hear?'

I was about to turn, but his hand was already on my

shoulder. Ripples of sensuous pleasure stirred my whole body yet the stubborn streak in me refused immediately to relax. He pulled me firmly round to face him.

'I suppose Mrs Maddox has been talking,' I said, trying hard to keep my voice and manner cool and controlled.

'She certainly has. And not before time. I hear you're –'

'Yes,' I interrupted, sharply because I was suddenly too excited and nervous to appear my natural self. 'I'm with child, Owain, so it's going to be all right for you after all – if it's a boy, of course. And I have a feeling it will be. Aren't you pleased? You should be. Maybe you've not made such a bad bargain after all.'

'Bargain?' He frowned.

'Well, that's what it was, wasn't it? You married me for that reason, to have a son. Why you should have taken the risk I don't know, after what you said about my mother. But, of course, there was a dowry, and you'd lost Eleanor –'

'Stop it.' Any hope of softening in his face that there'd been when he first looked into my eyes after entering, had turned to chill disappointment, or perhaps 'disillusion' was a better word to use. I wanted to cry wildly, passionately, 'No, *no*. I didn't mean to speak like that. I want to forget all the horrid things that have happened. I love you, Owain, and I want our baby terribly – *terribly*. We can begin again now, can't we? It's not too late, and I'm not really a virago.' Ah, yes, I wanted to blurt it all out – expose all the mixed feelings and desires that had been churning up in me for so long. But it was too late.

Releasing me abruptly he said with cold irony, 'How aptly you put things, Olwen. I congratulate you, not only for fulfilling at last your wifely duty, but for your efficient manner in dealing with the business side of our contract. However, I must insist that in the meantime you behave in a manner not likely to harm the birth of our future offspring. Otherwise, my dear, think and do whatever you please. And I shall do likewise.'

I stared at him, refusing to believe at first he could speak with such chill remoteness as though we were complete strangers.

But it was true.

And the next moment he had gone.

X

Autumn came gradually that year, a nostalgic golden period, filling the mountain lanes with the heady scents of fallen leaves and damp undergrowth under thin mists. Berries shone from scattered hedgerows and the lean dark branches of crouched trees. Away from Llangarrack where men were busy about the fields harvesting, a curious quiet brooded over the countryside. Owain followed the routine of his daily existence almost as though I did not exist, except to remind me to see I had regular physical checks at the doctor's in Abergavenny, and that I was responsible for bringing a healthy child into the world. He also commented on the increasing fragility of Merionne's appearance, and ordered me one day to take her with me the following week when the next appointment was due.

I did this. Owain drove me there himself, and after both myself and my daughter had been examined insisted on hearing the verdict for himself. We learned that I was in splendid form. Merionne, though, was delicate and needed all the fresh air, tonics and happiness and freedom that was possible. Her heart and lungs were not good. When pressed by Owain, the doctor admitted that her prospects of reaching maturity were doubtful. He could arrange for a specialist to see her, of course, but he was confident the verdict would be the same.

It was.

And from that day, following the departure of the highly qualified medical man from Llangarrack, love flowered in me once more for the child of sadness, Bryn's child who had been conceived so heedlessly on that far-off occasion in trust and innocence with all the beauty of the world bright about us.

Well, she was still beautiful; lovely as some delicate winged creature, a butterfly or silver moth flitting through sunlight and shade; doomed, it seemed, to an existence as brief. The next one, my son, would not be like that. I *knew* it by then with all the instinctive knowledge of maturity and approaching motherhood. As he moved and kicked within me I was assured of his strength, and a will to live inherited from two people, however antagonistic to each other, that would survive and flourish. I pictured him often in imagination, tall and sturdy, with Owain's bold features and fiery eyes. My colouring perhaps and black hair. I would call him Ithel after one of the ancient legendary Kings of Gwent. Owain, I thought, could hardly object, being so fanatically Welsh.

There were so many things we could have talked about together during those months and weeks of waiting; but the cold rift continued between us, and I frequently blamed myself bitterly for the harsh unwarranted way I'd spoken when I'd admitted my pregnancy. Why? *Why*? I asked myself helplessly many times. There was only one answer; nerves. I'd been so afraid of showing my true feelings in case Owain would scorn and reject them. I'd hoped desperately he'd realise the truth in quieter moments of retrospect. But obviously he never had. There was no subtlety in him, and from the start of our marriage he'd been suspicious and resentful, armed to think the worst. Any tenderness in his character now seemed concentrated on Merionne; as for passion and love – if his obsession could be termed love – then Eleanor had all he could give. Whether they met still or not I didn't know. But every time I took a walk up the lane, and the doctor had insisted that excercise was good for me, the tower stood dark and menacing in its tangle of undergrowth as a symbol of dark treachery.

I couldn't understand Merionne's passion for it. It was her delight, at four years old, to go wandering there, and Owain no longer seemed to object.

Neither did Mrs Maddox.

'The child has a touch of magic about her,' she said, 'like that thin grey creature that's always following her around, the dog. No harm's come to either from visiting there and that's a good sign; for some folks say the tower was one of Jack-o'-Kent's haunts in far-off bygone times, and if his spirit's friendly, then only good can come of it.'

'Jack-o'-Kent? Who *was* he?'

The old woman thought a moment, then answered, 'A wizard 'tis said, who could work good or ill. When he was a youngster he could charm birds, mostly crows, away from crops and imprison them somewhere, any old tower or barn, until harvest was safely done. He had a horse too. A fine black steed that could gallop so swift and high it covered roof tops. All stories, of course. Yes, indeed. Legend; but the little maid has a sense for other things than the world we live in.'

Remembering the curious carving over the entrance to the tower I mentioned it saying that I'd noticed the shape of a winged bird entwined in curious lettering. 'It could have been a crow,' I said. 'How odd.'

She shrugged.

'Perhaps. Perhaps not. No one's likely to know now. And maybe I shouldn't have mentioned 'Jack'. It's possible he never lived at all. So don't go getting fancies just because I let my old brain go wandering. You look to practical things and taking care of yourself. The little one too. Merionne.'

I did my best – mostly. But with the anticipation of such sturdy young life ahead, the increasing fragility of my beautiful little daughter frequently upset me to such an extent I could hardly bear to look at her. And when I did it was to resent the approaching advent of Owain's son. I felt guilt for past days when I could have shown more patience with the innocent sprite who through no fault of her own had been unable to communicate with the ordinary everyday world.

I allowed her more freedom, while taking note of the direction she took on her wanderings, realising Owain had been right when he'd said to me one day, 'Leave her the freedom she wants to go her own way. Her world isn't yours. So long as you've an idea of her whereabouts no harm will come to her.'

'Because of the dog, I suppose?' I'd said, with mild sarcasm.

And he'd replied, 'They're two of a kind. There's an instinct between them. He'll protect her.'

I'd thought at the time he was talking nonsense. But gradually I realised he did seem to possess a sixth sense of Celtic awareness. Day by day I was realising aspects of Owain's character I'd never remotely guessed. He could be at one moment so stern and hard, the next sensitive with compassion – a quality he mostly managed to hide under his rugged exterior. If only I could touch that core of softness and bring it to full life so its quality could break the ice of our relationship! – ah, how different life could be! At rare moments I caught a certain brief flame in his eyes when they turned on me, a relaxing of the tight lips when I thought with a leap of the senses he was about to make a gesture, utter one single word which could take me to his arms, and the bitterness would fall away, crumble in the realisation of our own deep need for each other.

But it never came.

And when the tentative expectant moment had passed I'd know it was Eleanor he wanted – always had, and always would. And my heart would be chilled and numb with disappointment until commonsense took a grip of me and turned my attention to other more practical things.

The period of waiting to give birth became heavy and wearying to my body, although I remained healthy, and was able to take reasonable walks each day. The late autumn weather continued curiously still that year, enhancing the rich colour of the valleys, and deep blue summits of the mountains above the purple slopes.

Gorse still flamed, and in the early mornings and evenings frail mists spread veils over the landscape.

It was on such an afternoon that Merionne strayed off on one of her wanderings.

Previous to her disappearance I'd noticed Owain cantering down the lane past the bottom of the drive, as though he'd returned from the vicinity of the tower. As usual the old suspicions rose in me that he'd been either meeting or on the watch for Eleanor Tripton. Trying to dispel a wave of jealousy with cynical acceptance of the situation I made an effort to concentrate on other matters – including Merionne.

She was nowhere about, and although little rambles on her own had now become almost habitual, I was uneasy. There was nothing about the weather or the day itself to cause apprehension. The sky was comparatively clear, windless, with only a very faint haze dimming the sunlight. But the niggle at the back of my mind continued. 'She'll be back presently,' I told myself stubbornly. 'She's gone off on her own many times before. This occasion's no different.'

It was though. If Owain had met her he'd have brought her back with him surely? I knew she'd have accompanied him willingly. He remained still her idol, the one person who could rouse her from her dream-like existence. Owain and the dog.

I'd seen the dog earlier in the day lurking, a grey shape against the shadows of the mountain above Llangarrack. Suppose it had lolloped off and the little girl had followed? Supposing she'd stumbled and fallen near that brooding pool, pit, or ancient quarry – whatever it was?

I called her name but there was no response. I hadn't really expected any. She never did these days, pay any attention to me.

Time passed. The light began to fade perceptibly, taking with it any rustle of wind there'd been through leaves and undergrowth. The stillness to my tensed nerves seemed ominous. I listened, with ears keyed, on the alert for any sound or sign of the child's whereabouts.

There was none. Only the faint murmur of the nearby stream trickling over the stones in a constant rhythmic gurgle that held to my distorted fancy the sinister quality of mocking laughter.

I wished Owain was with me. His ridicule of such absurd fancies would have helped. I could have born scolding and irritation; anything would have been preferable to the sense of isolation engulfing me. The early evening light was beautiful but sad somehow, the tall ferns and heather browning now, perfectly static as I made my way up the lane, calling intermittently, 'Merionne, Merionne, where are you? Come, darling. Merionne!' It was like crying into a void.

Breathless, heavy with the weight I carried, I paused. And then I heard it: the shrill eerie shriek of an animal, followed by the growl of another – or was it thunder breaking? I pushed on, hand on my heavy stomach, towards the tower. From dead silence all seemed creaking and breaking about me, the pounding of hooves and yelling of something else, something I couldn't distinguish. In a rush of actual terror I recalled Mrs Maddox's stories of 'Y Fall', the devil creature haunting the pool beyond the tower; but of course all that was nonsense. Nonsense, *nonsense*, I told myself as I started to run, stumbling and almost falling at times over stones and rough ground. Legends were just made up to frighten people. Nothing could harm Merionne but her own innocence and incapacity to recognise natural dangers such as bog, cliffs, and sudden precipices lurking round bends of the mountains.

That comparatively brief trek to the tower seemed endless. But at last I reached it, and after wiping my eyes clear of damp and perspiration stood facing its sinister frontage looming dark, almost black from tangled briars, gorse and heather. A dying sudden streak of sunlight slanted across the strange symbolic carving of the crow entwined with grotesque lettering, which for a second were starkly visible but meaningless to me. Then quickly the light flickered downwards and I saw it – only yards ahead. The white still form of a child. A girl. She was lying in crushed undergrowth, silver pale hair spread about her caught in briars and fallen leaves.

'Merionne,' I cried although my voice sounded only as a hoarse whisper, 'Merionne –'

I pushed ahead where thrusting twigs and vegetation had been trodden leaving signs of a rough track. There were other marks too, of hooves or paws in the earth, though I didn't notice them at the time, only my child, my own daughter, lying cold and still as a marble effigy with a twisted alder tree behind her at the side of the macabre dark ruin.

I bent down and touched her. She was still warm, but only just. Within me the new life stirred. Panic filled me. I didn't have to be told she was dead. There was a faint red mark across her neck. A scratch, I wondered, or – oh God, oh God! Somehow I managed to pull myself to my feet. I must get help. Owain – oh, if only Owain was here. But he'd ridden off somewhere, and the stable boy was no use. Mrs Maddox! I must hurry to the house and tell her; she'd know what to do. Perhaps after all it was only a fit of some kind – a faint. Perhaps – in those few frightening moments a heap of wild possibilities raced through my mind, although beyond at the back of them truth registered; I should never see Merionne alive again.

I made one attempt to lift her. It was no use. The earth seemed to sway beneath me, and I was temporarily faint. When I'd recovered I returned in a daze to Llangarrack and gasped out my story to a shocked Mrs Maddox.

At first she made no reply; then after a pause in which she forced me down into a chair and brought a glass of spirit from the cupboard, she said, trying to sound reasonable and unafraid, 'Now what's all this you say, mistress? The little one, Merionne? You say she's up there *dead*?'

'Yes, oh, yes. There's no mistake. I'm sure she is. But *why*? *How*? I touched her but –'

'And didn't she stir? Was she cold?'

'Not absolutely. It wasn't only *that*, though. It was the look of her! so small and – remote. Almost not real at all –'

The old housekeeper got up from her chair, reached for her stick, put on her shawl, and told me in over-firm tones, 'I'll not believe it. Not until I've seen for myself. And you, mistress, if you've the energy and will enough, see the boy has the trap out. He can bring it along soon as it's ready, and maybe catch me upon the way. Whether the poor little thing's still alive or not she'll have to be brought back, and the master's away to Abergavenny on business. So take hold of yourself, mistress. Whichever way it is must be accepted, and your place is to rest up and try to see reason. Fretting isn't going to help the one you're carrying. Your business is to see no harm's come of the shock you've had. Yes, indeed.'

I wanted to return with her, and yet I didn't. I protested against her command, but she turned on me in a fury, speaking wildly in Welsh so rapidly her words were incoherent.

I stood a moment watching her ancient figure flapping like some great black bird to the lane, then went to the stables and ordered the groom to get horse and trap ready. Slowly, I returned to the shadows of the kitchen and held my hands to the fire in an effort to bring warmth to my chilled nerves and body. Waiting, waiting, yet dreading to hear the rattle of wheels down the lane bearing all that was left of my lily-white child.

It was then that Owain walked through the door.

I turned my head as he approached, rigid, just staring at him. I suppose the fear must have shown in my face.

'What is it?' he asked. 'What's the matter?'

'Merionne,' I answered in a whisper. 'She's –'

'Lost?' he said, 'Is that it?' He grasped my shoulder, then forced my chin up so my quivering lips and wide frightened eyes told him more than any words could have done.

He let his hand fall to his side limply, walked to the window then returned to me quickly. 'You must tell me,' he insisted. 'At *once*. Out with it. *What's happened to Merionne?*'

'She's – she's up there, by the tower. I've been looking for her and calling, and then I found her. Lying in the bracken. I'm – oh, Owain! it was too terrible. She wasn't breathing. Wouldn't open her eyes. No movement, nothing. I tried to carry her, but it was no use. I couldn't. She's dead, Owain, *dead*. My Merionne.'

'*Yours?*' he gave the semblance of a bitter short laugh. 'What did *you* care about her?'

'I did. I *did*,' I cried, shocked. 'You can't blame me. You mustn't. Lately I've tried so hard with her. But –' Words failed me. I let myself sag limply into a chair.

'All right,' he said, 'don't carry on. Hysterics won't help. Where's Mrs Maddox?'

'She's gone to see. And I've sent the trap.'

'An old woman? On her own?'

'She insisted, and wouldn't have me with her. I *wanted* to, but then –'

Owain reached for a rug lying on a bench. His face was set, grim, expressionless, except for a twisted look of pain about the mouth.

'You don't know she's dead,' he said. 'Maybe she's had a

shock or fit of some kind. Have the kettle ready, and hot bricks for her bed. I'm off there.' He strode to the door.

'Can't I —'

'*No*. Do what I say. You understand? Act like a woman and show commonsense for once.'

He slammed out, leaving me shaken and cold; so cold it was as though the baby might turn to ice in my womb. I stirred presently, forcing myself automatically to do what I'd been ordered to — see the kettle was boiling on the hob, the fire freshly stacked with logs, and hot bricks ready to wrap in wool for heating her bed.

How long it was before the sad little procession returned I had no way of telling; my mind was so bleak and confused with the whirl of thoughts and questions consuming it. Was I to blame, was I? Could I have done more for the tragic little girl who had been born so beautiful but completely lacking in senses to face the realities of life? Or was it mostly Owain's fault for failing to love me and provide the necessary background of a happy marriage?

There was only one answer.

Bryn.

On the day of my 'awakening' with him, the seeds of tragedy had been sown. It was not Bryn's fault. I'd blamed him in my heart for a very long time. But he'd been, in the end, just a victim of nature, as Merionne's birth had been, perhaps even as Owain still was, in his bondage to Eleanor Tripton.

The tower had been the climax to everything since my marriage.

How I hated it.

Looking back fleetingly I wondered how the Widow Price would have exonerated her 'loving good Lord' for the terrible things that had happened. To me, as well as at Nanty-Clyd where all that I'd known as a child lay beneath a shining lake of water.

She would have managed it somehow, I thought wrily. Perhaps it was better to be born as she'd been – trusting in the Good Book as she'd been taught to do, just accepting because she hadn't the imagination to do otherwise.

With an effort to still my tortured restless conjecturing, I went to the door and looked up the lane. The dark shape of the carriage and its occupants was just appearing round the first bend of the winding lane.

I shuddered, knowing what else lay there.

*

Owain's face was very pale, grey-white when he carried her into the kitchen. Her head was cradled against his coat, fair hair falling in a stream of gold over his arm. Mrs Maddox followed, muttering lamentations in an undertone. The boy pulled a settle to the fire, and Owain laid her there, with cushions beneath her.

'Bring me a bowl with water in it,' he said, not looking at me, 'and spirit from the cupboard.' As I did his bidding he started rubbing her cold hand between his, and the fragile chest above the heart. He stopped every second or two to listen, and feel for any faint sound of a beat. When I brought the water and a cloth, he sponged her forehead tenderly, and the red scar on her cheek.

There was no movement or sign of life.

At last, after forcing whisky between the blue-ish lips, and putting his mouth to hers in the hope of reviving a pulse, he stood up, sighed, walked to the table, and with head bowed, said, 'Yes. Merionne's dead. Take her upstairs now, and lay her in the room that was to be hers later. Cover her with a quilt. But leave her face free. I'm riding for the doctor. He'll need an explanation, and I mean to get at the truth of what happened, and the reason for that cut by her throat.'

Without another word, Owain left, and as the sound of his horse's hooves died down the lane there was the faint roll of thunder from the distance. At the same time a frail breeze rose – ruffling the late leaves on the trees, soughing and sighing through bracken and bushes outside, driving its chill draught across the open door over the kitchen floor. A sad wind, like a requiem for the dead. Mrs Maddox rose and snapped the latch sharply. Its impact caused pale strands of Merionne's golden hair to quiver slightly. It was as though, for a second, the suggestion of life returned.

I knelt down, staring into her face. It was remote and lay pure and white as unsullied snow. An ice maiden. And that's what she'd been always, I told myself – a character from another world, reborn from a fairytale. And yet she had been *my* daughter, and Bryn's. Unprotected by us both. Only Owain had come truly to love her, and his love had risen from his passion for another, Eleanor. Could that be? Or had I misjudged him?

As always the eternal questioning ended only in torment. I was certain of nothing any more.

'Come,' I heard Mrs Maddox say, 'help me carry her – if you can bear to touch her.'

There was disapproval, even faint contempt, I imagined, in her voice.

I rose, and dumbly assisted the old woman to lift the child from the settle. So frail, so paper-light she was. Feather soft and limp against me. The stiffening had not yet set in. But I shivered. Death in any form depressed and frightened me; I was ashamed of my own weakness, but all I longed for during those agonising minutes of getting her upstairs to the bedroom so newly prepared for her, was to run from the house – run where living creatures breathed and flourished, where there was life still, and days ahead of sunshine and rain, warmth and contact with those who still had a future.

I suppose I was more shocked than I realised. But I managed to say to the old woman, 'It's all right. I can carry her alone. She weighs nothing at all.'

'In your state, mistress –'

'In *my* state?' I stared at her, and something in my gaze must have penetrated her stubborn mind. 'I'm *strong*,' I continued. 'Leave me. Sit down. I owe it to her.' I was talking at random, but it did seem to me in a queer kind of way that it was right, for once, for me to carry my two children together – the one who had gone, and the one yet to be born.

And this I did.

It was strange seeing the small golden-haired child lying in the pretty surroundings so recently prepared for her. Against the pale pink pillow with the flower patterned quilt spead over her she looked like a waxen doll among all the other symbols of childhood – animal pictures hanging on the walls papered with sprigged roses, a toy bear on a chair cushioned in pink, near a small light oak chest on a pale blue carpet.

There was a porcelain mug, too, with the name 'Merionne' on it. So many other small items chosen to please a child – and mostly by Owain. Stern, hard Owain, who'd brought something back each time he'd gone to a town on business. Why then when he'd spent so much thought concerning my daughter, couldn't he have given just a little love to me?

I tore my eyes away, too emotionally tired, drained and bewildered to watch or wonder any more.

And when I went downstairs again old Huw, the shepherd, was there. His long grizzled face held a look of scared foreboding. His mouth, above the jutting bearded chin, was drawn downwards between the deeply carved lines of furrowed cheeks, his eyes intent and staring under grey screwed-up brows. He was breathing heavily as though he'd been running, and his smock was torn.

'I came quick as I could,' he croaked, so harshly the words at first were hardly discernible. 'But it's a way from that steep hill. I had to cut down, see? Right round that bad pool place. It was above there I see'd it –'

'Sit you down, Huw, sit you down,' Mrs Maddox told him, urging him to a chair. 'A mug of ale's what you need. What we *all* need maybe after this – this terrible happening.' Her rusty voice broke, as she lifted her apron to wipe a tear from the corner of an eye. 'Now then,' as he did what she bid, 'tell us what you saw, man. It couldn't be worse than happenings here.'

'I know, I know. I feared it ma'am. The little child. It was her, wasn't it? But up there – and with the mist about comin' up – 't'warn't easy at first, to make out everythin'. Only the scream and that great black animal gone mad takin' the woman with it. But not before a streak of light showed things clear, only for a second mind you, but enough, enough! just as though the good God in his heaven'd sent a flame to shame the devil's work –' He paused to regain his breath and take a gulp of ale Mrs Maddox had brought him.

He wiped a bony hand across his mouth, shook his head woefully, closed his eyes briefly, and muttered, 'I see'd it.'

'What did you see, Huw?' I asked, dreading the answer.

He looked at me and began again with renewed energy.

'From the height I was at, and through that blindin' flash of light, I seed the woman come from the tower just as that tiny critter, the little child, crept out of the bushes, flickerin' like some butterfly critter against all that darkness – the dark woman with the pale hair and the black horse waitin'. Astride him she was, quick as lightnin'. Then – then I'm sure, sure as my name's Huw Thomas, she seed the child and lifted her whip an' struck her –'

'*What?*' Mrs Maddox's voice was a shriek. 'Struck little Merionne?'

'If *'t'was* young little miss, yes ma'am.'

'And after that?' I whispered.

'Ah.' That one word was an expression not only of fear and awe, but gratification. 'Then judgement fell.'

'Go on, go on, get on with it – tell us; speak you, Huw Thomas. What happened? The master will be back in no time at all. Better we know before it.'

The old man nodded.

'He'd been there himself at the tower, and that's the truth, mistress, but on no bad business I c'n take my oath on that.'

'Have done with your oaths and get on with your story,' Mrs Maddox persisted.

'Ah, well – it was the dog in the end. The dog that did it.'

'Did what?'

The old man lifted his face then, and for the first time the semblance of pleasure softened the hard lines.

'Vengeance,' he said. 'The vengeance of God against Y. Fall. Ah! – it was a wondrous sight. Wondrous and terrible. Out of nowhere it came, a lean grey thing, leaping at the animal's flanks, here, there, everywhere, with the black horse rearin' and poundin'. And then off they went, the two o' them, horse and rider and the grey dog followin'. It was a mad sight, I'm tellin' you. A wild ride to hell. But it was the little maid, *your* little maid I was thinkin' of when I took off down the hill. "Somethin's happened to her," I said speaking to myself. Bein' alone as I am gives you a knowledge of such things. "Somethin' not good. I must get to Llangarrack," I thought. "Master will be there. He left before *she* – the pale woman on the black horse. Master should know." So as I said, off I came –'

'Yes? Yes – out with it –' I heard the housekeeper saying impatiently. 'What else happened, man?'

Looking Mrs Maddox straight in the eyes, the old shepherd said slowly, 'It was at the pool. Y. Fall got them, both.'

'*What?*'

'That wild crazed creature of a horse went straight over and in. The woman was thrown. I had a quick look, no more. She was lying on the rocks at the side, cut an' bleedin' an' twisted like the devil himself with his crouched crook-back and hooved feet. Oh, I'm tellin' you it was a grievous horrible sight indeed. One I never thought to see in all the long years of my life.'

There was a pause in which I struggled to get the old man's story clear in my mind. In that awed shocked silence only the crackle of logs registered with the first steady drops of rain spattering the window, heralding a storm ahead.

At last old Huw asked, 'The little maid? Shouldn't somethin' be done?'

'It's been done,' Mrs Maddox told him. 'She's lying upstairs on her new bed.'

'Alive?'

'No,' I cried, with undue vehemence. 'Dead. *Dead* like a little bird, with a noose round its neck.'

Suddenly the tears began to fall; I could no longer contain them.

Mrs Maddox approached and put an arm round my shoulders. 'There, there, child,' she said, 'for that's what you still are, in spite of everything. Weep, girl, weep. It'll bring release from pain and ease the hurt.'

I swiftly came to myself, ashamed of showing such weakness.

'No, it won't,' I said fiercely, rubbing my eyes, 'nothing will. And I'm not a child. I'm Merionne's mother and Owain's wife. It's I who should be doing the comforting. Rest yourself, Mrs Maddox. Where's Dilly, by the way? And the other girl?'

'They had the day off, if you recall mistress, to go to the fair Abergavenny way.'

'Perhaps it's as well,' I remarked, 'although if I hadn't been busy with things here I might have seen Merionne slip away, and this dreadful thing wouldn't have happened.'

'Something would have,' old Huw predicted doomfully.

'From the start I had dark feelings 'bout that haughty woman over the hill. Yes, indeed – indeed I did. And the little maid so sweet and lily-pure.'

To escape his dire prophecies and murmurings I left him with Mrs Maddox, and walked down the drive to the gates which had been left open for Owain's return with the doctor.

Twilight had darkened to dusky evening, with lights already dotting the shadowed valley, blurred by blown rain. At intervals growls of thunder rumbled from the distance. I drew the shawl closer round me and waited for the familiar clip-clop of hooves from the valley below. And as I stood there the cool wet air seemed to release and wash some of my tension away. At last it came – the sound and sight of two riders emerging up the dimmed grey lane.

Owain dismounted when he saw me. 'What are you doing, Olwen – out in this? The rain's quite heavy now.'

'Better the rain than the gloomy kitchen,' I told him.

'Hm, come along then. There's no time to be wasted, and the doctor's wet.'

'Don't worry, ma'am,' the portly little figure answered me. 'I'm used to it and my business here is more important than a few drops of rain on my cape.'

I could have told him his presence was really unnecessary, since he could do nothing for my child. But the short formalities had to be endured, I knew, and in ten minutes the sad process of examination was over, and the doctor was in the parlour with Owain and I, taking a neat tot of whisky.

'Sad,' he said. 'Very sad. But I doubt the little thing could have reached maturity. Poor lungs, and a defective heart, too. Then –' He shrugged spreading his hands in a gesture of negation, 'as she was – in her condition of mind I should say – she'd have been a constant responsibility, and liable to go at any time. Try and look at the tragedy as an escape perhaps. Hm?'

I glanced at Owain. His expression was unfathomable, bleak.

'She had beauty and happiness in her,' he said.

I winced.

'Ah, well,' the doctor resumed, 'without health they can bring nothing but sorrow, Master Geraint. And she didn't suffer. She must have gone like – a flicker of candlelight, shall we say!'

'How do you know she didn't suffer? That mark on her neck – could it have been caused by a whip?'

Now what made him think of a whip? I wondered.

'It could. It could, sir. Or a bramble. But it didn't kill her. Shock of some kind, I'd say. Her heart gave out.'

At this point I said in as matter-of-fact way as I could muster, 'Perhaps you should hear what Huw, our shepherd, has to say. He's in the kitchen.'

'What has it to do with Huw?' Owain asked.

'You should soon know,' I told him coldly. 'Someone else *was* concerned in Merionne's death. Huw witnessed it.' In spite of my determination to keep any accusing note out of my voice, I was aware of a bitter triumph rising in me that had nothing to do with Merionne, a sensation I was later ashamed of, because, in spite of my dislike, even hatred, of Eleanor, I could never, in my right mind, have wished her dead.

Without more ado the two men went to the kitchen, and I went up to the bedroom once more where Merionne lay.

How long it was before Owain came to me I don't know. He pushed open the door, took a glance at the child, then went to the window and stood there, staring out through the sweep of rain over the grey hills.

I moved towards him quietly and touched his shoulder. 'Owain,' I said gently.

He jerked away as though he'd been struck. 'Don't –' The word, to me, had a bitter curt sound. 'Let's not be sentimental, Olwen. Useless. Quite irrelevant now.' He turned to face me. 'The doctor was right, maybe. It's an escape – for her, and – for *you*.'

'For *me*?' I was shocked.

'Of course. You've resented her for some time now. Quite natural, I suppose. She was a trouble and responsibility. Ironic, isn't it? In the beginning *I* wanted none of her. But I grew to care. She was so innocent. So –'

'Fair and beautiful. As beautiful as Eleanor Tripton,' I remarked acidly, remorselessly. 'Oh, I quite understand, Owain. I've known the truth for a long time. How you lay with her at the tower – how –'

'Stop it. *Stop* it.' A hand gripped my forearm briefly, so hard and tightly I could have screamed. 'What sort of woman are you? To be acting like any jealous fish-wife, when your own child lies – as she is – there on the bed. Look at her – *look* –'

I tore myself away. 'I've looked too long already, Owain. I can't stand any more, of you – of this place – or remembering –'

'But you *will* stand it,' I heard him say harshly, 'just as long as I wish. And when I don't, you can go, understand? Where and how you like.'

'I'm carrying your child, Owain, probably your son.'

'You can have him,' came the cold relentless reply. 'For this I've learned during the last months, Olwen March; at the moment I've no feeling for you or anything of yours, even if I bred him, you can both go to hell.'

Stunned, I watched him march through the door. There was a slam, and the sound of his receding footsteps along the corridor.

Then I fainted.

*

The next morning Owain was already picking at his breakfast when I went down. He was quiet and restrained, as though the experiences of the last days and hours had turned his nerves to iron.

Before I sat down, he pushed his plate away, got up and said in remote matter-of-fact tones, just as though nothing ill had passed between us, 'I'm off to Abergavenny to make funeral arrangements. It will be a quiet one, at the village church naturally. Is there anything you want from there?'

I shook my head. 'No, nothing.'

'You'll wear black, I suppose?'

'I've black clothes in my wardrobe. It would be stupid to waste money unnecessarily,' I remarked pointedly.

I didn't look at him, but was aware of his eyes fleetingly upon me before he left.

The day passed slowly by.

Owain was out until the evening. When he returned he told me he'd arranged for Merionne to be buried two days' later.

'No use dragging things out,' he said. 'The sooner it's over the better.'

'Yes.'

On the morning of the funeral all trace of the recent thundery weather had cleared, if only temporarily. The sun was shining, and the landscape looked achingly beautiful. A number of local people, including Mrs Maddox and the staff, had gathered, and after the sad little service, I noticed Harry Tripton moving away with the rest of those who'd attended to mourn — most, I guessed, out of curiosity. As Owain and I drove dry-eyed and rigid from the church following the committal, I broke the silence between us by asking, 'Did you notice Mr. Tripton was in church?'

'Of course.'

'Oh, I was rather surprised, considering –'

'As a neighbour he would be. It's customary.'

I was silent until my husband resumed, 'We shall pay the same respects to his wife, on Thursday.'

In spite of present grief a wave of resentment filled me, and later, back at Llangarrack I said, 'I must tell you now, Owain, I shan't be going with you to Eleanor Tripton's funeral. Apart from – other things – she was responsible for Merionne's death. I just couldn't.'

'We don't *know* that,' he said coldly. 'All we have is a garbled tale from old Huw who could have been imagining what he wanted to.' He was standing by the fire, a glass of whisky in one hand, and I was gathering my dark cloak and bonnet up from where I'd thrown them over the table after our return.

There was no anger in his voice, but his face was set, when he told me, 'Despite any distress you feel you'll accompany me, even if I have to drag you. But I'm sure that won't be necessary. You'll behave in a dignified and quiet manner, as befitting your social status and for the sake of the precious son you're carrying. And that's an order.'

'You can be so *cruel*,' I remarked bitterly. 'If you knew –'

'I know all that's necessary about you and your wild emotional suppositions,' Owain interrupted, 'and *more* than I want to concerning our ill-matched marriage. I'm not asking you to be reasonable or make an effort even to come to terms and start again. It's beyond you, and certainly I've neither the energy or taste for it any more! So I'm leaving. Don't worry, though. You'll not be abandoned or left without means. Everything will be arranged comfortably here for you during my absence. Then, when I come back to Llangarrack, if ever, we shall just have to see. No one can predict for certain what the future holds.'

'You mean – what *do* you mean, about going away?' I said in a rush. 'Only yesterday – Or was it the day before? It doesn't matter. You told *me* to go to hell, and the baby with me. Do you remember? Now you talk about yourself –'

He nodded. 'Exactly. A change of scene and company will suit me. I have the means now. An unexpected stroke of business luck. The mine is doing well, the accounts are up and stable. Some little time ago I made contact with a man who'll make an excellent farm bailiff. The days of scrimping and scraping are over, Olwen.'

I bit my lip, causing a minute spot of blood from a tooth prick.

'You haven't your land though,' I reminded him, 'your *Welsh* land that became Tripton's. When I first came here it was all you thought about, all you talked about, all you had us slaving and working for, including *me*. Do you remember? How I grubbed about fields pulling carrots and potatoes, and being at your beck and call always, never having a penny to spend, or allowed a free thought of my own –'

'Oh, I'm sure you had plenty of those, and the outdoor life seemed to suit you remarkably well,' Owain remarked with light sarcasm. 'You never went thin or hungry, if I remember, and there were always new clothes when you asked for them. Neither, it appeared, did you find our connubial existence distasteful. Indeed you seemed to flourish at such times. I should congratulate myself I suppose having provided, even briefly, an adequate substitute for Bryn.'

'*Bryn*! How contemptible of you, and at such a time.'

He suddenly relaxed. His shoulders sagged.

'Yes. I'm sorry.'

'I don't think you are,' I replied, trying to hurt him. 'I think you're only sorry about one thing – apart from Merionne – and *that's* that you'll never see Eleanor Tripton again.'

'Tit for tat, eh?'

'If you like. But you'd better accept one thing, Owain, I will *not* go with you to that – that woman's funeral.'

'And I say you will,' he said. 'If you don't there'll be talk, and your pride would suffer – badly.'

'I don't care about *pride*.'

'Oh, yes you do. Very much; and you'll need all of it, for the servants' respect alone, after I've gone.'

The chill ran through me again, icy and foreboding; heavy with a sense of loss ahead.

'And so you're not bothering about your grazing rights any more?' I managed to say, keeping my voice steady.

'It will come,' he said calmly, with no trace of emotion in his voice. 'I shall get it in the end, for the benefit of Llangarrack, if not myself.'

The distressing, almost intolerable, interview ended there.

I went upstairs, and flung myself on the bed where I lay, hands under my head, staring up at the ceiling thinking.

Thinking and trying to pinpoint exactly where matters had started to go so dreadfully wrong between us, and having to realise in the end that they had never been right. Bryn – Merionne – Eleanor – all gone now; but each in their own ways contributing factors of a disastrous union. Inevitably as the unhappy picture subsided, my troubled thoughts returned to the fragile child now at peace surely in the churchyard under the hill. Grief returned intensified. I got up restlessly, and went to the window. The bright morning sun was dimmed now by a thin haze of misted cloud. Everything was uncertain – hills, undergrowth and the silvered curl of the stream winding below. I glanced down, and just for a second caught the glimpse of a grey shape on the ground directly beneath the window. It sat staring upwards, perfectly motionless, two golden eyes gleaming. Their appeal – almost hunger – unnerved me. The grey dog.

For the first time something deep, deep within me responded. The pent-up emotions gave way.

In that short moment a bond beyond normal understanding was forged. But I knew also, that with

Merionne gone, I should never see the lone roving creature again.

Neither did I.

XI

Gentry from both sides of the border attended Eleanor Tripton's funeral – mostly English. I went grudgingly, but in the end had given in to Owain's compelling insistence, realising that to thwart him would provoke a scene that could very well endanger our marriage further. The whole business was distasteful to me; distasteful and frightening. Many times I had wished her out of the way – not dead necessarily, but at the very end of the world somewhere, where her taunting presence could no longer haunt our lives. Now all that was left of her lay in an expensive box. A box covered with flowers. But throughout the grim ceremony, I knew her living image remained hurtfully in Owain's mind. He stared straight ahead, controlled and dignified in mourning attire, betraying nothing – not so much as a quiver of an eyelash – of the memories and emotion stirring him. *I* felt them though, and the white knuckles of his fingers gripping the wooden pew, the clenched jaws and set unseeing stare of his eyes were proof enough, even if I needed proof, which I didn't.

In my stiff black silk gown, cape and bonnet, I felt ill-at-ease, a hypocrite. The smell of lilies and roses was sickening. There were moments when the impulse to leave the church – to rush away into the fresh air from the morbid scene which to me was mere mockery – almost overcame me. But closing my eyes briefly, I stayed by Owain's side until the last hymn, the last prayer and amen was said.

As we drove away, leaving any family and intimate friends to attend the committal, Owain remarked, 'There were a number of well-known folk present.'

'I suppose so.'

'I wonder what Tripton will do now.'

'Was she so important to his existence?' I asked tartly.

He frowned. 'What do you mean? She was his wife.'

'Oh, I was just thinking how often he was away.'

'That was *their* affair. To an astute businessman of his kind travelling around's frequently necessary.'

'You speak as though you admire him.'

'I admire his stubborn perspicacity, that's all. If we Welsh had one half of it we should have more acknowledged status in Britain today.'

'Oh, well,' I retorted, tired and bored, 'what does it matter? I'm glad it's over, anyway. The funeral, I mean.'

'So am I.'

I knew he was. Knew he'd only turned to topics of a practical and business nature to help erase poignant tormenting memories of Eleanor's beauty, Eleanor's passion and vibrant personality from his mind. *Would* that happen, in time, I wondered, or would she always remain for him as an elusive phantom of the past – as perhaps Merionne, in her childlike way, might? Certainly they would never be entirely forgotten; both in a terribly tragic way were so entwined in a pattern of doubt that neither could be entirely exorcised. Owain would never know for certain whether his mistress had been responsible for the death of my daughter, because the only witness had been an ancient shepherd who'd maintained Eleanor had used a whip. But the old man had been a distance away, and the mist had been rising. Merionne's heart had been weak. Oh, there was no factual proof. But *I* knew it, in my heart deep down, just as I realised that the grey dog had sprung at the horse and its rider in an effort to protect the little girl.

'A weapon of the Good Lord, perhaps,' I thought cynically, and I pictured the scene as it could so easily have been – the whip raised to strike the little girl, who'd followed Owain on his horse to the tower. Hearing voices she'd probably secreted herself well-hidden in the bushes, and when he'd left crept out to find who his companion had been. Eleanor had seen her, and outraged at what she considered the child's impertinence, had wildly used the whip.

Maybe the whip hadn't killed Merionne. But the shock had, and the grey dog had leaped in vengeance.

Yes, my picture – the *imagined* picture could so easily be the true one, although Merionne might have seen more. If Eleanor and Owain had been lying there together –

I refused to think further, shuddered that her innocent eyes could have been so bewildered by a scene I'd frequently pictured myself.

And I was ashamed of my own thoughts.

The past was past. Let it be.

'Please, please,' I prayed to whatever deity there was, 'don't take Owain from me.'

It seemed my prayers weren't answered.

Two days following Eleanor Tripton's funeral, my husband told me arrangements for his leaving Llangarrack for an indefinite period had been concluded.

'I'm off tomorrow,' he said.

'*Tomorrow*? Where?'

'Ireland, Brittany – I've important business in Brest. Shipping and other things.'

'But –' I tried to protest. The words just wouldn't come.

'There's nothing to bother your head about. You knew I was going. I didn't speak lightly, too sharply, perhaps. But you should know by now I never mince words. We have to be apart, Olwen. For quite a time.'

'What does that mean?'

'Weeks, months, a year – it all depends.'

'A *year*?'

'Perhaps. That should give us both time to get things into perspective. Whether we come together again depends. At the moment I'd say it seems highly unlikely. However –'

'And your son, when he's born? Remember what you said? He and I – we could both go to hell? Where exactly is hell on the map?'

He gave a sardonic smile, holding as well a hint of pain.

'Wherever we choose to make it. Either of us.'

I sighed, and shook my head hopelessly.

'I don't understand. If I gave you my solemn promise never to mention the word Bryn again, and you –'

'I wouldn't believe you. And I wouldn't want to put pressure on you that much. Oh, for Heaven's sake, Olwen, let things be. I'm sorry and that's that. You've nothing to worry about. Dai Morgan will make an excellent bailiff. He'll have complete control of things here, and in case of emergency I've arranged with Mrs Maddox how to contact me if necessary.'

'An address, you mean?'

'*Contact* I've said.'

'And I am to have none? Don't you realise how humiliating that is for me?'

'No. You're not the type to be humiliated. Out of sight, out of mind. You'll soon forget about me. Especially in view of the nice little income waiting for you in the bank.'

Feeling outraged, wanting to thump and beat my hands against his chest, to scream, 'How *can* you? How can you? You wanted me once, you *know* you did, when you held and kissed me and took me in passion. We've quarrelled and fought, but the wanting and desire was always there, wasn't it? *Wasn't* it? In spite of Eleanor and her sly ways. I hated her from the first moment, and I hate her now, although she's dead. I do, I *do*. It may be wicked, but I love you, Owain –'

Oh, yes, I wanted to shout all those things, break somehow the terrible cold determination in his voice and his eyes. But I didn't. It would have been futile. So giving up at last I said calmly, 'Very well. I suppose you'll have some slight interest – sufficient to want to know when the baby's born. I presume Mrs Maddox will forward the information?'

He smiled wrily.

'Olwen, your lady-like presumption is quite correct. And I do congratulate you on your civilised manner of putting things. You've learned quite a deal during your years at Llangarrack.'

I flushed and turned away, muttering, 'In more ways than one.'

He left me then, and I did not see him again that day until the evening. Our meeting was by chance. Feeling the atmosphere of the house stifling I'd taken a longer walk than was usual, wandering as usual up the lane past the tower, and impelled perhaps by a morbid curiosity cut up the path leading leftwards towards the sinister deep pit, quarry, or tarn – whatever it was – where Eleanor had taken her last ride to her death.

Everything was static and grey – the lean dark trees empty of leaves now, the lowering sky above the rocks and entangled undergrowth encircling the glassy sheen of water, with the brooding shadowed hump of mountain beyond.

I walked slowly, apprehensive of the lingering atmosphere of recent tragedy which in the complete silence assumed an identity of its own, more compelling than any moaning of wind or storm would have been.

And then I saw him. The figure of a man staring into the depths of the chasm, so unified with the rest of the scene that I might not have noticed until he moved; just a slight lift of the head. But it was enough.

Owain.

My first reaction of surprise, almost shock, changed painfully to a strange sense of sadness and resignation. Hopelessness engulfed me, for myself, and for him, who could not keep his grieving to himself, but had to come to the scene of tragedy to relive his memories of the woman he'd longed for so desperately.

For the first time I forgot myself, my jealousy and resentment, and stepping as quietly as possible over the damp ground went towards him. He half turned. I lifted an arm and touched his shoulder.

'Owain,' I whispered, and when he said nothing, continued, 'please don't look like that. I know how hurt you are. But it's no good, she's gone. Come back with me, *please* come –'

I waited, holding my breath, hoping so desperately that he'd soften, and accept at that moment what I had to give.

But his only reaction was to say in unemotional tones, 'I was thinking of the horse. A fine animal. They'll never get him up, of course. Nor even try. It's a devil hole, this pit. Probably didn't suffer, though. I hope not. They've found pieces of his harness floating, but nothing else.

There was a pause. When I didn't speak he asked, 'Why did you come? What are you doing here?'

'I was out for my evening walk, that's all,' I told him. 'And when I saw you, I thought – I thought maybe you needed someone to talk with – about Eleanor, if you wanted.' Those last words were an effort, but I spoke them.

'Me?' He gave the semblance, or mockery, of a short laugh. 'Why me? It's Tripton, if anyone, who needs comfort.'

And probably Owain was right, I decided, with all pity turning suddenly to anger, at myself for even imagining I could be of help, and at Owain for his continued rejection of me. It was true that Tripton himself had been a victim. Tripton, her husband, to whom she'd been faithless for so long, in her constant liaison with the man I'd married. In a way I felt sorry for him, although despising his stupidity for having been so cheated and betrayed. Unless, of course, he didn't care. In any case, what did Tripton matter? He was nothing to me.

'I'll be going now then,' I said, knowing there was no point in staying longer.

'I may as well escort you,' Owain said, with a cynical attempt at courtesy. 'The ground's rough. Would you like my arm?'

'Don't worry,' I retorted quickly. 'I can look after myself. I'm well used to being on my own.'

'As you will.'

We walked back to Llangarrack in almost complete silence; a thin wind was rising, and spots of rain were already falling from the heavy evening sky which in the last hour had become overcast.

Once I caught my toe on a stone. A strong hand was immediately under my elbow, and Owain said curtly, 'You should be more careful. Look where you're going, especially now, at such a time and in your state.'

'Oh! what does it matter?'

'Don't be stupid,' he said shortly. 'And there's no necessity for melodrama. The funerals are both over.'

'And you have a new life ahead,' I stated with a coldness I was far from feeling. 'Owain, couldn't we –?'

Before I could finish, he interrupted, 'No, we could *not*. But it isn't the end of the world. You lost your chance with me through your insane jealousy, and I lost mine when I failed to act as I wanted by beating and spoiling you in the sound old-fashioned way. Now the initiative's gone. So just let things be, will you?'

I did.

Not another word was spoken during the rest of the walk back to Llangarrack.

For most of the night I lay restless and unable to sleep,

tossing about, listening to a wild torrent of rain beating round the house, driven on a high wind. Before dawn the storm eased a little, and I managed to doze fitfully. At about seven I got up, dressed quickly, and went downstairs thinking to see Owain before he left – hoping desperately that he might, even at such a late date, have decided afterall to postpone his departure.

But when I got downstairs he had already gone.

After I'd refused breakfast, in spite of Mrs Maddox's admonishment and pleas to 'Get something inside me for the sake of the two of us –' meaning myself and the unborn babe, she handed me an envelope. Just the one word 'Olwen' was written on it in Owain's handwriting.

With my heart beating quickly, aware of Mrs. Maddox's eyes on me, I clutched it firmly in my hand and took it up to the bedroom.

There, sitting on the bed, I tore it open, and read –

Dear Olwen,
    This is not a sentimental 'au revoir', I shall be back some time, as you well know. I have duties at Llangarrack and naturally will wish to see any future heir of mine when the time comes. Incidentally, I feel it's important you should know the true facts concerning my relationship to Eleanor. We had been lovers for some time before my marriage to you which was ill-starred from the beginning, and not entirely, though, *my* fault. Later, following your obvious distaste of my presence in your bed, there were two other occasions when I sought comfort and confidence through her. But *not* as you suspected on that tragic occasion of Merionne's death. I had been contemplating for some time on the possibility of having the tower renovated, and made practical for old Huw to live in – especially during the winter months, and had gone there that day for the express purpose of judging what

re-building was necessary. I found Eleanor already waiting for me when I arrived. Her horse was tethered near the entrance, which could explain, I suppose, why Merionne later was curious, and hid herself until I came out. I never saw the child, of course, or heard a thing. I couldn't have, anyway. The argument and scene between Eleanor and myself was vitriolic. By then, believe it or not, I was quite sick and tired of her possessive attentions. But she wouldn't go.

Oh, yes, I admit for years she'd been my obsession and wild dream. But I no longer loved her. She had become to me little more than an escape and weapon of revenge on that greedy English Tripton for snatching her away at the very last minute from under my nose, half way to the altar.

Love is a fancy word, and not one I use with ease. Where *you* were concerned I shied from it ever since that first occasion when I found you'd already been with a man. That Bryn of yours. I *did* love Merionne, though – not only because of her innocence, but because in so many ways she was like you – not dark and fiery as you are – but with your features and smile, and way of half dancing when you walk. *You* do that, did you know? Even in those silly pointed boots you wear. And in your wildness, too. Yes, she was wild just as you are. Fey is the word used, I think – although you wouldn't admit it naturally. *You* had so much more though – reality, and a zest for living and the flesh.

I think we might have been happy if we'd had sufficient sense to try harder. But in time, Olwen, constant argument and distrust lead to defeat. And I am defeated now; just as you are. Somehow in the vicious wilderness of our mutual existence, love has become lost.

I'm sorry, but that's the truth, and if you examine your feelings honestly, you'll know it.

Will it ever return?

God alone knows – if God does in reality exist at all. In the meantime I shall receive news of you through the channels arranged, and I hope you easily give birth to the son you want. I say *you* – because I personally have no feelings whatever now on the subject. My interest has dried up.

All the same, if you have any problems at Llangarrack, let Mrs Maddox know, and I shall be informed, and do the best to have them solved. My reason for giving you no address is simply that I don't intend to be pestered by letters or pleas to return.

Take care of yourself.

Owain.

P.S. You will think this a wordy letter from such a hard-headed, brusque character as myself. But remember – I am also Welsh, Olwen.

Another thing. About your mother – she was a highly respected young servant girl before that blackguard's desertion, and your birth. Later – well, things aren't easy for the poor without virtue or means to obtain a decent livelihood. Pity her, Olwen, and you'll feel better. 'O.'.

For some moments I stared mutely at the letter, trying to understand many things that before had puzzled me. Only one thing registered clearly. Owain had admitted that he had no love for me.

XII

The next few weeks were the loneliest I'd ever known, although I told myself I didn't care; Owain was just one person in a world of others – I was still young; with life ahead, and if he chose to go off wandering the world on his own, then so could I.

Once the baby was born.

The baby.

Sometimes I longed for him passionately, impatient for the time – not so very long ahead, when I'd be able to hold him in my arms. At others – though rarely – he loomed as a symbol in my heart of my bondage to a man who had no need of me at all except for providing an heir.

If the child was a boy I had no doubt whatever that Owain would be back at Llangarrack on the first opportunity. His denial of having any interest in any future son I might bear was not true. He had lied about that; to me, and perhaps to himself.

So the birth, which should not now be so very long ahead, would be the means of bringing the Master of the estate home!

As the days slowly passed, this knowledge deepened resentment in me. I didn't want Owain that way. I was no longer a very young girl in love; the time apart from him had revealed hidden reserves of strength, which, in spite of loneliness, enabled me to notice and appreciate other things: the deepening colours of autumn gradually changing from golden browns to misted winter greys and dark shadowed blue; the personal affairs of the household staff; being free to take the carriage when I wanted, to the village, and becoming a personality on my own in the district. I could also go into Abergavenny when I wished for shopping. Luckily I had no health problems or minor complications of pregnancy, and such practical social diversions prevented me from undue fretting. In fact, I stoically refused to fret at all, although underneath my calm exterior I was aware – bitterly so – of the greatest lack a woman can know – that of a husband's presence and affection.

Yes. Resigned I might be, but lonely still.

Because my days were so filled at that period of my life these moments of self-knowledge, luckily, were rare. And when they came, they were a torment.

In such a mood I went out one day in early December for a walk up the lane. The weather was cold. Frost rimed the hedgerows, diamonding the bare black branches of the trees with silver-white. I wore a thick woollen cape which I'd bought in a fit of extravagance on a visit to Newport. It was woven in a pattern of green and blue check.

'You shouldn've chosen something else,' Mrs Maddox had said, when I showed her later. 'Something from the real Welsh shop in that arcade there. There's not even a dragon on this, not anywhere. It should have a tiny mark – the true red dragon of Wales. This is a foreign thing. Ireland, or Scotland, maybe.'

'I don't care,' I told her. 'It's warm. Dear Mrs Maddox, you *do* sound a bit stuffy sometimes.'

'Stuffy? *Me*? What a word to use. Yes, indeed. It seems to me you're getting a little strange in your ways and tongue, mistress.'

'Well, that's to be expected, isn't it? At this important time of my life?'

I'd glimpsed at myself through the mirror as I spoke, and noticed for the first time since Owain's departure that much of the recent strain had left my face. My colour was rich and warm, my eyes bright and glowing, and the little dark green velvet bonnet I'd also purchased, suited the cape and the rebellious dark curls which *would* stray – however well they'd been pinned – against the smooth curve of my cheeks.

I looked well, and young, and comely, perhaps even beautiful; not at all the way most pregnant women were supposed to appear, fragile and forever on the point of fainting. Mrs Maddox had made some remark, but I didn't hear.

Just for a few moments I'd felt exuberant and suddenly happy with the possibility of a glowing future ahead.

The feeling was only brief, of course, to be followed by the sinking feeling and eternal question of 'what's the use? Owain doesn't care. If I wore sackcloth he wouldn't notice. And anyway, he isn't here.'

Aloud I'd said to Mrs Maddox, 'I expect you're right. Probably I shouldn't have spent the money.'

'Oh, now, don't go thinking I want to *criticise*, mistress,' the old woman had added in conciliatory tones. 'It's becoming to you, yes, indeed. And as you say warm. The dragon isn't really *that* important.'

But to her I knew it was.

However, knowing it suited me, although it was slightly long and would have to be shortened a little later, I'd put it on that certain afternoon, hoping to get some mental as well as physical comfort from it. I wore the little velvet bonnet as well. There'd be no one to see me, which was a pity. It would have been pleasant for a man's eyes to linger with admiration as I passed. With the garment's fullness billowing round me, even my full figure was hardly visible. Still, I told myself with an attempt at humour, there were always rabbits, maybe an odd deer or two, and birds hopping about the trees in search of late berries.

So I continued on my way, playing a defiant little game of 'don't care' with myself, pretending all was well and that everything would be wonderful in the future. The sharpening air was exhilarating. My head and feet felt light. I should have put on sturdier boots, of course. I could imagine Owain saying in his blunt condemning way, 'What a fool of a woman you are – soon to be a mother and tripping about like that. Absurd.'

Yes, it *was* absurd.

And I knew it a moment later when the narrow point of my patent shoe somehow caught on a stone, and due to the sloping ground and the length of my long cloak, I could not prevent myself from falling. A mere straight stumble might have done no damage, but I went at an awkward angle with an ankle and part of my body twisted painfully to one side. For a moment or two the shock stunned me. I tried to rise, but fell back in agony, clutching my stomach. It was then I felt a strong arm at my back and heard a voice saying – a man's – 'Don't move! Wait a bit. Are you hurt –'

In a daze I looked up and saw a stranger staring down at me. Even through my pain I noted a pair of blue eyes, and that his face was kind and concerned under a thatch of curling brown hair. I tried to smile and rise again, but the effort was too much and I was thankful once the first agony had passed, just to lie back, relaxing.

'I shall be all right in a moment,' I told him. 'My ankle's twisted, and – and ' A wave of faintness overcame me. He took off his coat, laid it over the crisp bracken, and when I'd recovered, said firmly, 'You need help. More than I alone can give. Where do you live?'

'Llangarrack,' I said. 'I'm Mrs Geraint. It's not far. My husband's away somewhere, but if you – if you go down the lane you'll come to the house – large and grey with a short drive at the front. Mrs Maddox, the housekeeper, will send the trap probably or get the doctor. I don't know – anyway there are servants, I'd be so grateful –'

He stood up. I saw for the first time that he was young, handsome, somewhat unconventionally but expensively clad in a grey cape-coat – an actor, perhaps. yes, that could be it. How very ironic that I *should* be seen after all in my new attire, but in such a sorry state, with the bonnet lying yards away, the cloak spread out revealing my swollen stomach and undeniably pregnant condition.

'I *am* sorry,' I managed to gasp. 'So silly of me, and undignified. But I think – I think perhaps – you ought to be quick –'

He sprang erectly to his feet, 'Lie still, then, try not to move. Just rest. I'll be back quick as possible –'

I watched him turn and race at astonishing speed down the lane until his figure finally disappeared round a curve leaving me exhausted and scared with the frightening knowledge intensifying during each fresh stab of pain that I would probably lose the baby. And tragically as it seemed then, that was exactly what happened, but not until the late evening. The doctor was present, and a midwife, located by the stranger who'd taken a horse from the stables and ridden straight into Abergavenny after assisting the groom to get me home, on an improvised stretcher.

I'd prayed it wouldn't happen – prayed and prayed, for Owain's sake, until I remembered through a haze of agonised memory that neither the child nor myself were wanted any more by my husband. Somewhere deep in the recesses of my brain – his bitter words had remained and festered beneath the facade I'd created for myself.

Well, it was over now.

I would not bear Owain's child.

Our marriage was now truly ended.

No more longing, or bickering or shame. No more jealousy or hurt. No hope, no love.

When I was better – and I soon would be, I was strong – I'd somehow, somewhere, plan another life, and I'd be a different person, because I knew now, what human beings could do to each other, and would be prepared. In the meantime, I'd just rest a bit, do in reason what Mrs Maddox ordered or implored for my health's sake. She'd contact Owain probably and give him the news, although I ordered her not to. Would he come? Perhaps. Perhaps not. I didn't care. By then it was at last true; I really didn't; neither did I enquire if the housekeeper had obeyed me or not.

Nothing mattered any more but myself.

I was *free*.

With a shrewd glance at me one day the old woman said probingly, 'You never mention the master these days, mistress. Have you no wish for news or a word from me maybe, that could give comfort?'

I shook my head.

'No, Mrs Maddox. What passes between you and Mr Geraint is your own affair. If he has anything to convey to me it must come from him personally.'

'Now, mistress, after what's happened –'

'After what's happened everything becomes more clear, doesn't it? Anyway, I don't wish to talk about my marriage or what lies ahead. For the time being I shall stay at Llangarrack. Later –' I shrugged. 'Who knows?'

'It's hard you've become all of a sudden,' Mrs Maddox stated disapprovingly. 'Losing that precious child as you have, and so quickly following the death of the other one, Merionne, has been a shock as well, I realise, so allowances must be made. Yes, indeed. But a softer heart would be more –'

'Becoming and appreciated by the Good Lord,' I interrupted ironically before she could finish. 'Yes, I agree. A very convenient philosophy, but one I'm afraid quite unacceptable where I'm concerned. I was brought up Methodist, to believe in a loving God, Mrs Maddox, but I must admit life hasn't done much to prove the truth of it. So please, *please* don't preach or scold. Just leave me alone, and let me think and live in the way I choose.'

After that she was silent.

A fortnight passed, and one afternoon a visitor arrived at Llangarrack with a bunch of roses in his hand. Roses – in winter. They must have cost quite a lot, and holding them was a young curly-haired man, the stranger who'd assisted me that fateful, painful afternoon of my fall.

XIII

From the first days of my friendship with Linden Gray, the stranger who'd come to my rescue on the afternoon of my fall, I was aware that his interest in me held a deepening warmth more significant than mere sympathy or wish to be helpful in a distressing situation.

During the few weeks before Christmas we learned much about each other. He was the second son of a wealthy landowner in Cornwall, I discovered, very much in his father's bad books because instead of following the career intended for him at the Bar, he'd gone his own way following university, choosing to try his luck as an artist. He had not actually been disowned by his wealthy sire, so wasn't without funds, but remained in bad odour with his family nevertheless. He was staying temporarily at a coaching house near Crickhowell, following a period of travelling with Circus folk, painting portraits of many colourful personalities which he intended to show later at an exhibition in London.

'I'm a roamer – always was,' he told me, during one of our early strolls together. 'City life wouldn't suit me, and I wasn't wanted on the country estate. John, my brother, has complete control. Anyway –' he gave me a whimsical smile – 'I'm not the controllable kind, and life at home would bore me. You know how it is. Hunting, parties, all the sociable how d'ye do of being nice to rich mamas of marriageable daughters. God! *what* a bore.'

'Yes,' I agreed. 'I suppose it must be.'

'Tell me about yourself,' he said, his very blue eyes staring down at me with an urgency in them, an intimacy I found mildly embarrassing.

'Oh – there's not much to tell,' I answered ambiguously. 'Just that I – I suppose I've been unfortunate in marrying a man who doesn't really care about me. It was arranged, you see, the marriage. And it hasn't worked. He's away now on business. When he finds out about the – what's happened, he may not come back at all. I don't know – it's difficult to look ahead and see anything clearly.'

'I'm sorry,' he said after a pause.

'I shouldn't be talking like this,' I remarked hastily. 'It sounds disloyal, doesn't it? But sometimes – well, I've a habit of letting things burst out before I know it. Maybe because there's no one to confide in. Mrs Maddox, the housekeeper, is very kind in her own funny way. But she's old, and Owain, my husband, is her pet, and darling. It's natural; she looked after him ever since he was born, you see. She tries to be fair; but – oh, let's not talk about *me*,' I ended abruptly.

'I think you should,' he insisted. 'Obviously, Olwen, you need a friend badly. And I should *like* to think – it would mean quite a lot to me if you could see me that way.' A hand took mine and pressed it warmly. I *should* have drawn mine away but did not. Impulsively I raised my face and smiled at him. I knew in that moment if I'd paused a second longer he'd have kissed me. The afternoon, despite its winter chill seemed suddenly warm and golden, and filled with youth and hope. But I made an abrupt movement, pulled myself away, and feeling my cheeks burn, said over-brightly, 'Yes, thank you. Of course you can be a friend. You became that the very first time when I was so stupid to fall, and you were there to help.'

'Probably it was meant,' he said meaningfully.

'Oh, no I don't think so. How could it be? It was awful. And tragic –'

'Yes, yes, forgive me. I do realise the tragedy. For any woman to lose a child –'

'I wasn't thinking of myself,' I interrupted. 'I was referring to my husband, Owain, Mr Geraint. I *am* still his wife, you know.'

How stilted and silly the words sounded in my own ears. And why couldn't I take a little pleasure – enjoy a sentimental dalliance that was obviously waiting for me if I wished to take it? There was no reason at all for refusing, considering Owain's behaviour towards me. So fortifying myself by defiance of the convention, I added quickly, 'Don't think me a prude. I'm just –'

He laughed. 'Just virtuous, and extremely, tantalisingly, desirable,' he added, 'and with spirit enough to show me I mustn't jump my guns. You needn't explain. I understand the situation very well, Mrs Geraint – Olwen. So we'll wait and see for the time being. I certainly wouldn't press my attentions where they weren't wanted. But that husband of yours, you know – he needs a good hard shock, if you ask me, or a kick in the – forgive me – not in front of a lady – but you know what I mean.'

Unexpectedly I giggled.

'Yes, I know, Mr Gray. And you're very impudent.'

'Linden, if you please. As a mere friend even, surely first names are permitted.'

To which I agreed with a brief smile and nod, and managed then to turn the subject to more impersonal matters, such as the mysterious beauty of the mountains, farming in general, and his successes and failures so far, as a roaming artist.

From that point the relationship between us gradually deepened. Most days, when the weather allowed, he rode over to see me, and on one occasion he came by hired chaise to take me out for lunch at the inn.

I wore my best velvet blue cloak over a silk gown of the same colour in a lighter shade purchased before I'd known of my pregnancy. It was still quite up to date, and although my figure was slightly fuller than it had been, the fit was perfect, even more alluring than it had previously appeared, showing the full curve of my breasts to advantage, and enhancing the clear cream quality of my skin and shining lustre of dark hair.

Mrs Maddox was bluntly disapproving.

When I came down the stairs she said harshly, 'I can't understand you, mistress. So recently bereaved, and your husband away as he is! It isn't *right*, not right at all. No, indeed. Whatever will he think and say when he comes back? He'll get to know of this, mark my words. And then –'

'He probably won't come back whilst I'm here,' I answered her coldly. 'He hasn't even written to me since the miscarriage. You informed him surely what had happened? You must have done.'

'True enough.' Her lips tightened. 'And a message back I had. A message saying as long as you were all right he'd leave your welfare to me. "She wouldn't welcome me just now," he said, "if I thought I could be of use I'd be back at Llangarrack on the first opportunity. As things are it's better I stay away." These are the very words he used, mistress. Know them by heart I do.'

'How very convenient for you both,' I remarked tartly.

She flushed.

'If you were *my* daughter I'd know what to do,' she said, hardly able to control her anger, 'and it's something the master should have done long ago. Now don't you get on your high-horse, mistress, and tell me to mind my own business. That's what I'm doing and will continue to do, while I bide at Llangarrack, and that'll be for some time yet, God willing.'

She gave another angry glare at me then stumped away into the kitchen.

I smiled briefly, then made my way to the door, hearing

the chaise approach. Nevertheless, I was slightly discomforted, and my heart was beating more quickly than usual. The truth was I felt in my bones that some sort of crisis was approaching.

What? I didn't know.

But the next night I did.

*

The luncheon served at The Goose and Crown was excellent but I realised when I entered the panelled dining room on Linden's arm that I might appear over-dressed, which Mrs Maddox had certainly thought me. There were only a few visitors eating there – most of them soberly clad, residents perhaps, including a portly ageing gentleman in a wine coloured jacket who glanced at me appraisingly with rheumy eyes as I passed. Regular daily frequenters of the inn I supposed were probably taking wine or spirits in the Bar Parlour or tap-room, which was perhaps as well, for I felt mildly discomfited already by the obvious interest shown in my appearance.

That is until I was seated at the table allotted, with my bonnet removed and cape draped over the back of my chair, and saw the beaming look of admiration on Linden's face. Instantly my spirits rose. For so long I'd been criticised and put in my place – it was pleasurable to be appreciated as a woman – especially by one so handsome, young, and courteous, as Linden Gray.

Of course, our meal together was only a light-hearted interim and I knew it. The two pleasant hours passed as a kind of dream in which I became briefly quite a different person from Olwen Geraint of Llangarrack. It was rather like seeing myself in a play, knowing that at the finale everything would be over, and I should be back in the real world again. For a moment I must have looked serious; perhaps my thoughts showed on my face, for Linden said quietly, suddenly solemn, 'You look beautiful, Olwen.'

Truly. I'd like to paint you.'

I felt the colour rising warm to my cheeks.

'Me?'

I was lifting a wine glass to my lips. He stretched out and gently held my wrist so I had to place it down.

'Yes. Just like you are now,' he said, 'wearing that dress and with the half-shy, half-expectant look in your eyes. I could paint a masterpiece if you'd allow it.'

I was not only doubtful, but bemused.

'You're joking,' I said. 'You must be. I'm not at all the type of woman for a portrait. There are some on the walls at Llangarrack – very dignified and imperious-looking. And *I'm* not, a bit; I'm just –'

'Unique and natural and lovely,' he broke in. 'I really mean it, darling.'

'And you mustn't call me that,' I told him sternly. 'I have a husband, and you and I hardly know each other. Probably I shouldn't even be lunching like this with you – I'm sure I shouldn't, really. Not after what happened, meeting you the way I did. No, *please*, Mr Gray –'

'Linden,' he reminded me.

'Linden, then.' I paused for a moment, and after toying with the wine again added, 'We must be sensible.'

'Why?'

The blunt question took me aback.

'Because it's – Because we *have* to be. There's no point in pretending things aren't as they are. I've enjoyed – I'm still enjoying being with you, and having this lovely meal together. It's done me good. But –' I sighed. 'Oh, I wish I could make you understand.'

'I do. You have a husband who treats you abominably; you've gone through quite a lot, and he's heaped more suffering and loneliness on you. From what you've said, and what I've gathered, he's a bit of a cad content to go his own way without a single thought in his mind for *your* feelings. You've already admitted you'll probably never

---

live together again. Then what *are* you going to do, Olwen? Have you thought? You're young and beautiful. With me we could –'

'No. *No*,' I said insistently, though in hushed tones for fear others should hear. 'Please don't go on. If you do I shall have to get up and leave. *Please*, Linden.'

He shrugged, looked down at his plate, then agreed grudgingly, 'Very well. As you wish – for the moment. But the portrait. Surely you won't deny me that? I could come tomorrow to Llangarrack and paint you in that old-fashioned parlour, staring through the window, with the light on your face. In the same dress, the one you're wearing now, and the cape half off your shoulder. Yes – that's how I picture you – everything else dark, except your own radiance –' He broke off, the whimsical smile warm about his mouth again.

'But there's Mrs Maddox. She'd think it *dreadful*. Terribly wrong. Imagine all sorts of things.'

'And is she your guardian?'

'Of course not. I'm mistress of the house. You know that. But she's old-fashioned. She doesn't trust men – especially theatre people and artists.'

'Then we'll just have to show her she can, won't we?' he remarked disarmingly. 'She can lurk about, peep, pry, even open the door at times to see there's no wicked seduction act going on. I can assure you, Olwen, I'll behave decorously, and leave without casting even the faintest shadow on your virtue and loyalty to your unpleasant spouse.'

He was so insistent, so buoyant, with such a disarming manner of proving his argument, that I at last gave in, and when he said farewell later at the door of Llangarrack it had been arranged for him to call the following afternoon with painting materials, and easel, to make a preliminary sketch.

Mrs Maddox was astounded and aghast when she heard, throwing up her hands in dismay.

'A *painter*? At Llangarrack? Do you really mean it, mistress? And in the master's absence? *No*. I'll not believe it. He's up to no good, that young man. I knew it when I first set eyes on him. Today was bad enough, seeing you drive off like any loose woman would, but to have him *here*! And you alone together. I won't have it, no indeed. Indeed I will not.'

'You can keep away safely in the kitchen if you wish, Mrs Maddox,' I said coldly. 'It's hardly your place to tell me what I should or should *not* do. I'm sorry to have to speak so, but there's no wrong at all in having my portrait painted; I've promised Linden. And that's that.'

'*Linden*. So it's Linden now.'

'Quite a nice name,' I said pertly, more confident of myself now the news was out. 'Easy on the tongue.'

'Well I don't know, I'm sure. Indeed I don't. All I can say is, I hope the master never hears of it. Yes, yes, that I do.'

Shaking her head dolefully she retreated to her own premises.

The next afternoon Linden arrived on horseback, looking more than ever like some character out of a stage play, wearing a cape, and with his painting gear and slender easel securely strapped on his mount.

From the window I watched him dismount and tether the horse to a tree.

Moments later there was a rap at the door which Mrs Maddox ignored. In my blue dress I left the parlour, and lifted the latch myself.

He entered, and I smiled with anticipation, realising that I was actually looking forward to the painting session ahead.

Never, in my wildest dreams, could I have imagined how it would end.

XIV

'This is only a preliminary sketch,' Linden remarked as he studied me, thoughtfully, brush in hand, from his easel, which he'd placed some yards away so the light was clear on his canvas, yet in such a position, he said, to define perfectly the modelling of my face.

I was seated, as he'd previously suggested, with the soft blue velvet cape draped over one shoulder, leaving the other free, skin visible above the low cut sleeve of my gown.

I had my hair loosely pinned and threaded with a blue ribbon, one curl left free against a cheek.

'I'm afraid I'm not very good at sitting still,' I told him before he made the first strokes with his brush.

He smiled.

'You needn't be. I want you to be quite natural. Prattle on if you like, tell me more about yourself – of your first days at – what was the place called where you lived with your dragon of a foster-mother?'

'Nanty-Clyd,' I answered, 'and she wasn't a dragon at all. She was quite kind in her way, dutiful, and did her best to bring me up in a proper manner.'

He made a comical grimace. 'Oh, *duty*! Such a fearsome boring word. Weren't you ever bored, Olwen?'

'Sometimes,' I admitted. 'It was *having* to do and believe what I was told to, about life, and being good, and behaving well. I'm afraid I wasn't very good at behaving. But then there *were* other things –' I broke off reflectively, remembering, with a spasm of old pain, Bryn, the

179

mountain and blue butterflies, Marged, and the vicious old goose, Polly the Post – oh, how long ago it all was, and yet just for a few moments they seemed so very near again and real, until I recalled that they had all gone, and now lay deep below the shining lake that had claimed so many lives.

'Yes?' I heard Linden questioning. 'You said "other things". What other things, Olwen?' He was watching me closely, at the same time working rapidly, trying to catch something, I suppose, of sadness on my face.

'Oh, just people,' I answered enigmatically. 'It was so long ago. And remembering isn't always happy.'

'No.'

There was a silence for a considerable time, then he said, 'Just keep your head as it is now, for a minute, and with your eyes looking the way they are, as though they were searching for something, then you can move as you wish. All right?'

I nodded, and did as he wanted.

'Good.' He gave a sigh of satisfaction. 'I really believe I've captured a – a certain quality, shall I say, already. This may not merely be a sketch after all. It's like that sometimes. From the very start the first impression of a portrait can hold a subtlety never realised again, like –' He paused, then continued 'Like the light and shade of nature, a fleeting awareness of hidden secret things suddenly revealed. Do you understand?'

I did, and I didn't, at the same time. Linden Gray certainly had a rich imagination and way of talking which stirred and touched my heart like music, though I could never have put what I felt into words. Elusive.

At one point I was reminded of the slipping shadow of the grey dog that had vanished so inexplicably during the weeks following Merionne's death. Had it truly been real? Ever? Yes, yes, it must have been, because Mrs Maddox had seen it, and Owain. 'A creature of the mountain,' he'd said more than once, and 'it had mountain knowledge.' But then Owain was Welsh, true Welsh. And my heart ached that I'd never deeply understood him or delved properly beneath the granite exterior to the emotionally hungry Owain so beloved by Merionne. I'd been too hurt myself, and too jealous of Eleanor Tripton to make a single selfless effort at understanding.

As always in arguments with myself, I went from one extreme to the other. The truth was, I told myself firmly, no one was either completely good or bad. If I could have been more commonsensical! – but I never would be, I knew that, just as I knew during that brief wandering of my thoughts, that I had still the capacity to love Owain deeply if I ever had the chance.

I must have smiled a little, because I was brought back to reality by Linden saying, 'Now what is it?'

'What do you mean?'

'You had an almost unearthly longing in your eyes – just as though you were searching for something beyond your reach, but still utterly enthralling and desirable. There was a glow about you.'

'Oh?'

'But not for me. I'm astute enough to know that. It's true, isn't it, Olwen?'

'Mr Gray,' I answered. 'Linden, I hardly know you, do I? But I've accepted you as a friend, and I like you very much. I'm really honoured that you are painting me; but –'

'I know. I know. Your heart is elsewhere. However badly he's treated you, you're in love with your selfish, overbearing husband. That's the truth, isn't it?'

I didn't answer, but bowed my head ever so slightly.

'Well, I hope he'll appreciate it one day, and that you won't be too old or harried then to clutch what happiness you can before you die. I doubt it, from what I've heard of him. But for *your* sake, Olwen, I do truly wish the miracle to come true.'

I said no more than a quiet whispered 'thank you'. And after that Linden started to paint again, with, it seemed, added fervour and dedication.

Time passed.

The light was beginning to fade, when it happened.

There was the sound of heavy footsteps outside. Then the grating of a door opening, followed by another.

I glanced back across the room, simultaneously with Linden, and there he stood. Owain himself unsmiling and set-faced as ever, yet with a hard self-controlled dignity about him that set my heart racing and brought the wild blood to my face.

I jumped up and ran towards him.

'Owain –'

He lifted a hand and brushed me aside, walking straight to the easel where he snatched the canvas from under Linden's very nose.

'So you did this?' His dark eyes, cold yet fiery were intent on Linden's blue ones.

'As you see, sir, but it's only in the first stages yet. So I don't expect you to admire such an early impression of your lovely wife. However, if I may have your permission to continue with one or two more sittings I've hopes you may come to appreciate it eventually.'

'Your hopes endorse your infernal impertinence,' Owain stated coldly, with the dangerous undertone in his voice I knew so well. 'You come here in my absence, uninvited and take the liberty of using her as a model without so much as a request or permission from myself or my housekeeper. You have, in short, been making hay, as they say, whilst I was away from my own home. If I hadn't learned also of the help you gave during Mrs Geraint's accident, I would kick you out here and now. As it is –' He thrust a hand into his pocket, drew out a number of coins and pushed them forcefully into the other man's hand. 'Take these for your effort. I'll keep the painting. But don't show your face here again, sir, or you'll regret it.'

I made an ineffectual gesture of protest, but it was ignored. Mutely I watched Linden Gray place paints in his box, gather up the easel, and crimson-faced, without a glance in my direction walk to the door. He paused there, turned and said ironically, 'Good luck to you.'

Then he was gone.

Minutes later I heard the sounds of horse's hooves galloping down the drive. Owain watched from the window, then turned to me, and said, 'Now, Olwen, I think the time has come once more for a little talk, don't you?'

The same old words, I thought ironically. How many times had he spoken them before? It didn't matter. This time would be different.

'Yes, Owain,' I answered, lifting my head high, my eyes firmly confronting him. 'Where and when would you like to begin?'

'Immediately,' he said. 'And upstairs, because it happens you have quite a deal of explaining to do.'

'You also,' I told him.

He didn't answer, but I was aware of a gleam of surprised admiration in his eyes as I swept before him in my blue gown, into the hall, and up the stairs to the bedroom.

XV

I went to the window, sighed, then turned to face him as he closed the door quietly and came towards me. He looked strained and tired, but not so angered as I'd feared.

'Sit down, Olwen,' he said indicating the chair by the dressing table. 'I shan't eat or beat you. I'm trying to be civilised. But why did you do it?'

I obeyed, then asked:

'Do what, Owain? Allow a young man to paint me in my own parlour? A young man who might easily have saved my life? No one knew where I was that day, on my own. If he hadn't come along –'

'I know. I *know*. And I'm not blaming him for taking advantage of the incident to start a titillating romance afterwards. Not very commendable of him, but understandable under the circumstances.'

'What do you mean by that? The circumstances?'

'Look at the mirror and see for yourself. You're a very beautiful woman.'

Was I? I stared at the reflection softly shadowed by the glass, and knew what he said was true. My eyes appeared enormous fringed by thick dark lashes, my lustrous hair, tumbled slightly from combs and ribbons, waved becomingly against the pearly cream of cheeks and neck.

How I'd changed, I thought, recalling the naive outwardly prim and frightened young creature who'd been deposited so unceremoniously those years ago on the threshold of Llangarrack. And yet in some ways I was still the same – bewildered and uncertain of the future, longing for the security of a strong man's love possessing me, with the capacity to hold me safe from straying.

'Well?' I heard Owain ask.

'What do you want me to say?'

He came up behind me, placing both hands on my shoulders. The dark brooding eyes reflected above my own were compelling in his lean face. I could feel the breath of him, a warm drift over my hair. He was near. So very near, all the hidden pulses of my body stirred in longing. Yet I dare not move lest the spell of those few magic moments was broken and lost again for ever.

Then he cleared his throat, shattering the silence, and asked bluntly, 'Do you love me, Olwen? Has there ever been a time when you felt a spark of it for me in your wayward heart?'

I turned my head staring upwards in astonishment.

'Me? Love *you*? Owain, what a – what a question. When –' I broke off, quite unable to finish.

His hands dropped away.

'I must apologise,' he said stiffly. 'Maybe I shouldn't have asked.'

'No, you shouldn't, you should have known better,' I retorted, 'and you must realise it, if you think back. The question should have come the other way round, from *me* if at all. You never showed that *I* mattered at all except for – except – oh, Owain, you make it so difficult. If I really thought –'

'What?'

'It was always Eleanor,' I dared to remind him, 'and you were so brusque and cold to me. Sometimes I could hardly bear it. I know *I* was nasty, too. But that was because I'd tried so hard to wipe her out of your life, I mean. And I just couldn't –'

'I explained all about Eleanor in my letter,' he said, 'and if you'd had a grain of sense in your lovely head when you'd read it, you'd have puzzled out the truth for yourself. But enough of that. I would like a reply to my question after all.' And he repeated, 'Do you *love* me?'

Then all resistance went from me; I jumped up and almost before I knew it, was in his arms. 'Oh, yes, oh, yes, *yes*, Owain darling. I always have – well, perhaps not *always* – but for a very long time. You should have *seen*, understood. But you were so proud, haughty, and forbidding –'

'And you were such a damned little vixen,' he said, holding me so close I could hardly breathe. 'It seemed every time I spoke or looked at you you were spoiling for a fight. And there were times I admit when I was tempted to give you a downright good spanking for being the wicked little chit you were.'

'There were other things,' I told him, 'when I pleaded with you and you just wouldn't listen.'

'Quits then,' he agreed.

'Not quite,' I said, pulling myself from his arms.

'What more then?'

'It's your turn, isn't it?'

He looked puzzled.

'Mine? Turn? What about?'

'You haven't said it yet, not once, that you feel the same – oh!' I broke off impatiently. 'That one word you've always shied from where I'm concerned – L.O.V.E. Owain. *Love*.'

He smiled then, and the years fell from him as he said gruffly, with a kind of wonder, 'I love you. I adore you – cariad, sweetheart, you're the one good thing that's ever happened to me in all my life. It's what drove me away – though I didn't know it – because I couldn't stick the bleakness of things between us – and what brought me back, when I heard what'd happened – just to show you.'

'Show me what?' I asked, puzzled.

'That it was *you* I needed. By then neither the son, the heir, Llangarrack or anything else counted in comparison. If we ever *do* have a child – *right*! He'll be cared for and given every chance in life I can afford. But you come first. And if we don't have a family I shan't be bothered, and it's the truth I'm telling you.'

'We shall though,' I said confidently. 'I'm sure of it.'

He lifted me up in his arms then, and carried me to the large bed where he'd taken me before in male lust, lacking the one quality that could create beauty of physical passion, and purity from mutual need.

Now all was to be different.

And while he unbuttoned my gown at the throat and breasts, kissing and letting his lips linger on my flesh as he did so, I knew, from the solemn, still searching look in his eyes, there was yet something to be solved between us. I helped him to remove my petticoats and frilly obstructing underwear, and when we were both ready, man and woman waiting for fulfilment, he bent over me and spoke gently, but with a demanding urgency in his voice:

'Olwen,' he said, 'you must tell me. I have to know something – even if the truth makes me jealous as hell. You understand? I'm not by nature a soft forgiving type of man, but at this moment in time, believe me, however hard it is, I could forgive you anything provided you come out with it, fair and square –'

'What is it you want to know, Owain?' I managed to say in the steadiest voice possible.

'Was there anything between you and that *heroic* artist fellow I'd a mind to knock flat, when I saw him mooning over you? Tell me, anything at all?'

'No, Owain, nothing. We just walked and talked a bit and had a meal together at an inn near Crickhowell. Very expensive, I know. But the food was good. I enjoyed that.'

I watched, staring at him as a glint of humour lit his eyes. 'Well, well!' he said, 'that means I shall have to dig into my own pocket and go one better. Quite an achievement for a mean-minded man like me.'

I didn't answer; there was no need.

His lips were on mine, his body hard against me. As he took me to him what glimmer of light remained faded to darkness and the throbbing wonder of a man and a woman unified for the first time truly, in the sanctified peace and warmth of requited love.

*

The next day, in the afternoon when Owain was out on some business of the estate, Mrs Maddox, looking extremely surprised, came into the parlour where I was sewing, to tell me a visitor was at the door waiting to see Owain.

'It's Master Tripton,' she informed me, 'from over the hill. I said Master Geraint was out, and it was then he asked if it would be convenient to speak with you. So what is it I shall be saying then?'

I pushed the sewing into my workbasket quickly. 'That's quite all right,' I told her. 'Show him in, Mrs Maddox.'

A minute later Eleanor's husband entered, looking tired, a little harassed, and considerably older than on the occasion of his rare visits to Llangarrack with his wife.

'Forgive me if I'm intruding,' he remarked. 'But I have here something important for your husband, and would be grateful if you would give it to him when he returns.'

'Why, certainly,' I answered.

From an inner pocket of his jacket he produced an envelope with Owain's name on it. 'Inside,' he said, 'is a legal document cancelling any past bet concerning lands previously held by the Geraint family which were taken over to the Tripton estate. The document has been signed by me and witnessed by my solicitors. It is lawful and irreversible.'

I hardly knew what to say except, 'But that's kind of you, Mr Tripton, and my husband, I know, will be very grateful.'

'Oh, well!' he shrugged. 'I've no need of it now. Those acres were always a bit of an embarrassment. Anyway, I'm leaving this evening. I've arranged for the estate to be sold. Without Eleanor none of it matters. I shall be off to a change of scene and pastures new, the quicker the better as far as I'm concerned.'

He studied me carefully before adding, 'I know very well what many other folk said of her, and I knew what was going on – I should have been a fool not to. But –' he shook his head slowly, ' – to me she meant everything. I wanted her just as she was, headstrong, wild, selfish, immoral if you like, but *honest*, Mrs Geraint. And beautiful. My God! what a beauty she was.'

'Yes,' I agreed, knowing my voice must have hardened perceptibly.

There was a softening of his bluff features when he continued, '*You* have no cause for worry. You're well-matched, you and Owain, and believe me he'd had no interest in Eleanor for a very long time. You'll pardon me for speaking so, I hope. Another thing –'

'Yes, Mr Tripton?'

'All this rivalry there's been between myself, the Triptons and the Geraints – it's stupid really, when you come to think of it, because in the end the good earth belongs to itself only. Any dividing line is a mere fallacy, just as it is with the Welsh and English. We're all *folk*. Human beings, my dear; we need each other, and the sooner we come together the better.'

He held out his hand and grasped mine warmly.

I took it with a strange sensation of humility that was new to me.

He was right, the Englishman. So very right.

But I doubted Owain would feel the same way.

He didn't *quite*, when I told him. But he was more magnanimous and moved than I'd anticipated. 'Oh, he wasn't a bad sort of fellow,' he agreed condescendingly. 'This document proves it. He'd a conscience about it, I suppose. On the other hand he held on to it as long as it was of use to him.'

'Can't you be charitable for once,' I queried, 'and admit

you'd probably have done just the same if you were in his shoes?'

'Maybe. Maybe. But I wasn't, thank God. I was born Welsh, and Welsh I'll remain to the end of my days. My heritage, Olwen.'

'Yes,' I agreed. 'And mine.'

He smiled, and placed an arm round my waist, murmuring, '*Ours*, and those that come after us.'

Together we walked to the window. Snow was beginning to fall, and between the black, white and misted deep blue of the landscape I fancied I glimpsed the graceful form of a deer – or was it a grey dog racing towards the high ridge of the mountains?

It could have been my imagination, of course. But I like to think it was more, a sign perhaps that all was well with Merionne, where she lay sleeping, and a herald of good for the future Owain and I had together.